BEDTIME
STORIES *and* RHYMES

BEDTIME
STORIES *and* RHYMES

Selected by

Alistair Hedley

Illustrated by

Kate Aldous, Sue Clarke, Claire Henley,

Anna Cynthia Leplar, Jacqueline Mair, Sheila Moxley,

This is a Parragon Book
First Published in 2000

Parragon
Queen Street House
4 Queen Street
Bath BA1 1HE UK

Printed and bound in Indonesia
ISBN 0 75254 459 4

Contents

ANNA BANANA

Anna Banana
Played the piano;
The piano broke
And Anna choked.

LUCY LOCKET

Lucy Locket lost her pocket,
  Kitty Fisher found it,
But not a penny was there in it
  Just the binding round it

LITTLE MISS MUFFET

Little Miss Muffet
Sat on a tuffet,
Eating her curds and whey;
There came a great spider,
Who sat down beside her,
And frightened Miss Muffet away.

BAA, BAA, BLACK SHEEP

Baa, baa, black sheep, have you any wool?

Yes, sir; yes, sir, three bags full:

One for the master, one for the dame,

And one for the little boy that lives down the lane.

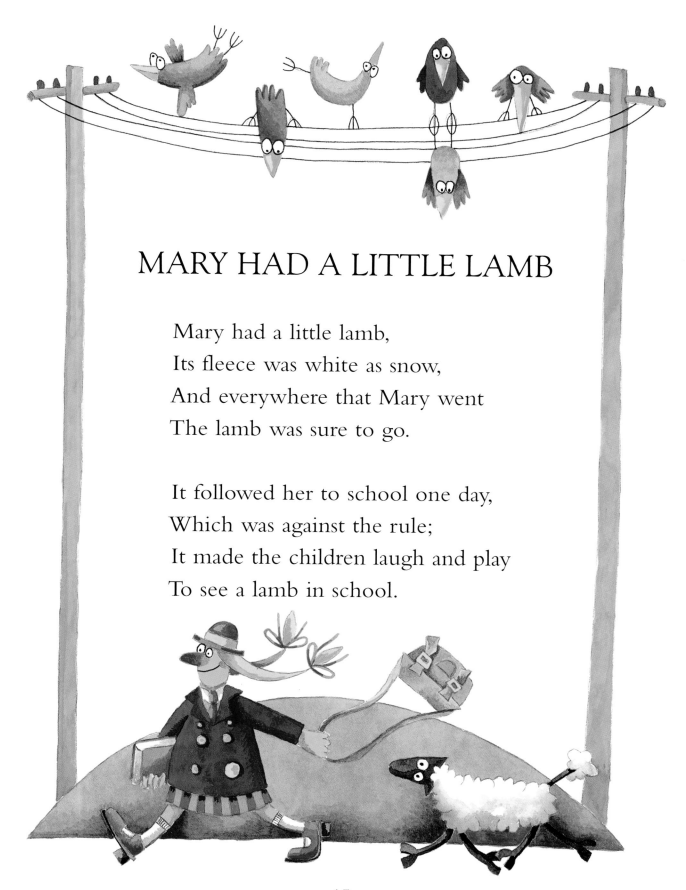

MARY HAD A LITTLE LAMB

Mary had a little lamb,
Its fleece was white as snow,
And everywhere that Mary went
The lamb was sure to go.

It followed her to school one day,
Which was against the rule;
It made the children laugh and play
To see a lamb in school.

THE MILLER OF DEE

There was a jolly miller
    Lived on the river Dee:
He worked and sung from morn till night,
    No lark so blithe as he;
And this the burden of his song
    For ever used to be—
I jump mejerrime jee!
    I care for nobody—no! not I,
Since nobody cares for me.

16

AS I WAS GOING ALONG

As I was going along, long, long,
A singing a comical song, song, song,
The lane that I went was so long, long, long,
And the song that I sung was as long, long, long,
And so I went singing along.

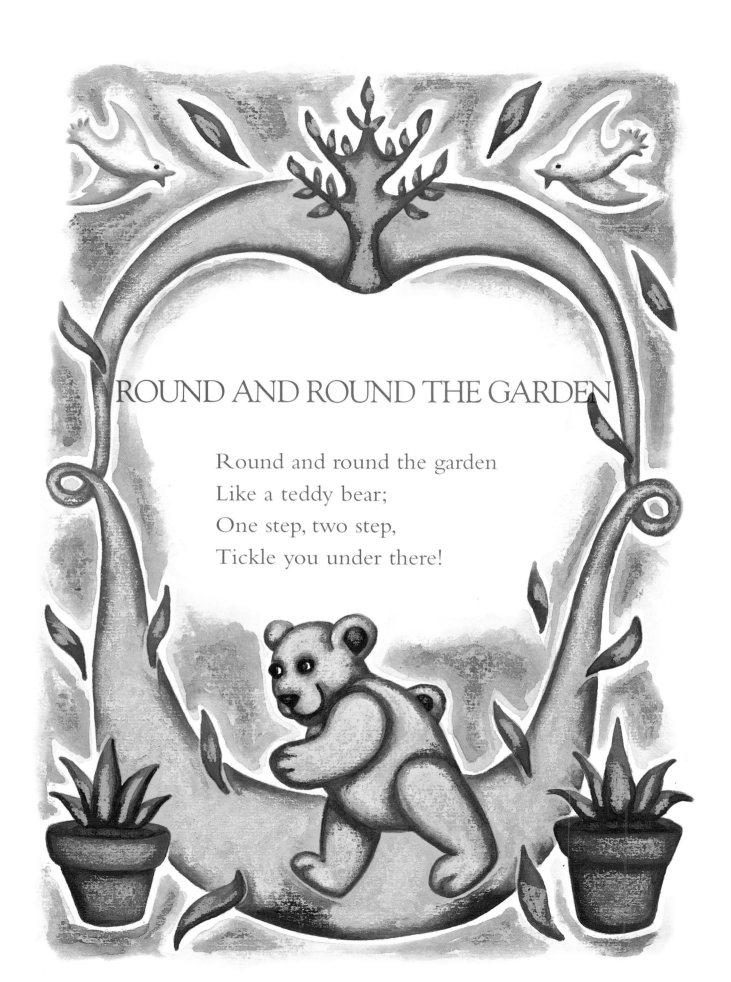

ROUND AND ROUND THE GARDEN

Round and round the garden
Like a teddy bear;
One step, two step,
Tickle you under there!

THIS LITTLE PIGGY

This little piggy went to market,
This little piggy stayed at home,
This little piggy had roast beef,
This little piggy had none,
And this little piggy cried, *Wee-wee-wee-wee-wee,*
   All the way home.

TO MARKET, TO MARKET

To market, to market,
To buy a plum bun;
Home again, come again,
Market is done.

TO MARKET, TO MARKET, TO BUY A FAT PIG

To market, to market, to buy a fat pig,
Home again, home again, dancing a jig;
Ride to the market to buy a fat hog,
Home again, home again, jiggety-jog.

20

THIS IS THE WAY THE LADIES RIDE

This is the way the ladies ride:
  Tri, tre, tre, tree,
  Tri, tre, tre, tree!
This is the way the ladies ride:
  Tri, tre, tre, tre, tri-tre-tre-tree!

This is the way the gentlemen ride:
  Gallop-a-trot,
  Gallop-a-trot!
This is the way the gentlemen ride:
  Gallop-a-gallop-a-trot!

This is the way the farmers ride:
  Hobbledy-hoy,
  Hobbledy-hoy!
This is the way the farmers ride:
  Hobbledy hobbledy-hoy!

THERE WAS AN OLD WOMAN
WHO LIVED IN A SHOE

There was an old woman who lived in a shoe,
She had so many children she didn't know
  what to do;
She gave them some broth without any bread;
And scolded them soundly and put them to bed.

THERE WAS AN OLD WOMAN
AND WHAT DO YOU THINK?

There was an old woman, and what do you think?
She lived upon nothing but victuals and drink:
Victuals and drink were the chief of her diet;
This tiresome old woman could never be quiet.

THERE WAS AN OLD WOMAN
CALLED NOTHING-AT-ALL

There was an old woman called Nothing-at-all,
Who rejoiced in a dwelling exceedingly small;
A man stretched his mouth to its utmost extent,
And down at one gulp house and old woman went.

23

WHEN I WAS A BACHELOR

When I was a bachelor I lived by myself,
And all the meat I got I put upon a shelf;
The rats and the mice did lead me such a life
That I went to London to get myself a wife.

The streets were so broad and the lanes were
   so narrow,
I could not get my wife home without a
   wheelbarrow;
The wheelbarrow broke, my wife got a fall,
Down tumbled wheelbarrow, little wife, and all.

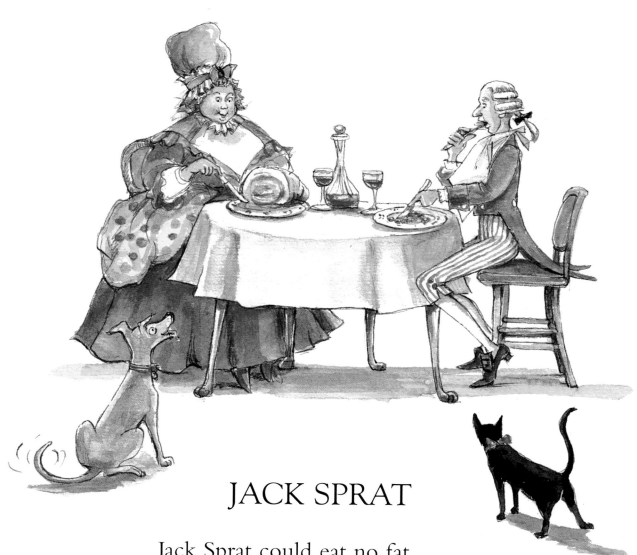

JACK SPRAT

Jack Sprat could eat no fat,
His wife could eat no lean,
And so between the two of them
They licked the platter clean.

MOTHER TABBYSKINS

Sitting at a window
In her cloak and hat
I saw Mother Tabbyskins,
The *real* old cat!
　Very old, very old,
　Crumplety and lame;
Teaching kittens how to scold—
　Is it not a shame?

Kittens in the garden
Looking in her face,
Learning how to spit and swear—
Oh, what a disgrace!
　Very wrong, very wrong,
　Very wrong and bad;
Such a subject for our song,
　Makes us all too sad.

Old Mother Tabbyskins,
Sticking out her head,
Gave a howl, and then a yowl,
Hobbled off to bed.

Very sick, very sick,
Very savage, too;
Pray send for a doctor quick—
Any one will do!

Doctor Mouse came creeping,
Creeping to her bed;
Lanced her gums and felt her pulse,
Whispered she was dead.
Very sly, very sly,
The *real* old cat
Open kept her weather eye—
Mouse! beware of that!

Old Mother Tabbyskins,
Saying "Serves him right",
Gobbled up the doctor, with
Infinite delight.
Very fast, very fast,
Very pleasant, too—
"What a pity it can't last!
Bring another, do!"

ELIZABETH ANNA HART

THE FROG

A widow was baking in her kitchen and asked her daughter to go down to the well to fetch some water. Off the daughter went, down to the well by the meadow, but when she came to the well she found that it was dry. She wondered what she and her mother would do without water, for it was high summer and there had not been a cloud in the sky for days. And the poor girl was so anxious that she sat down beside the well and began to cry.

Suddenly, through her sobbing, the girl heard a plop, and a frog jumped out of the well.

"What are you crying for?" asked the frog.

The girl explained that there was no water and she did not know what to do.

"Well," said the frog, "if you will be my wife, you shall have all the water you need."

The girl thought that the creature was making fun of her, so she went along with the joke, and agreed to be the frog's wife. She lowered her bucket into the well once more, and sure enough, when she pulled it up, the bucket was full of water.

The girl took the water back to her mother, and thought no more about the frog until it was evening. Then, as the girl and her mother were about to go to bed, they heard a small voice and a scratching sound at the door of their cottage: "Open the door, my own true love. Remember the promise you made to me, when fetching your water down at the well."

"Ugh, it's a filthy frog," said the girl.

"Open the door to the poor creature," said her mother, for she was a gentle woman who liked to be kind to animals. And so they opened the door.

"Give me my supper, my own true love. Remember the promise you made to me, when fetching your water down at the well," the frog went on.

"Ugh, I don't want to feed the filthy beast," said the daughter.

"Give the poor creature something to eat," insisted her mother. So they laid out some food and the frog ate it all up thankfully.

"Put me to bed, my own true love. Remember the promise you made to me, when fetching your water down at the well," said the frog.

"Ugh, we can't have that slimy thing in our bed," protested the daughter.

"Put the poor creature to bed and let it rest," said the mother. So they turned down the sheets and the frog climbed into bed.

Then the frog spoke again: "Bring me an axe, my own true love. Remember the promise you made to me, when fetching your water down at the well."

The widow and her daughter looked at each other in deep puzzlement. "What would the creature want with an axe?" asked the girl. "It is far too heavy for a frog to lift."

"Fetch him an axe," said the mother. "We shall see soon

enough." So the daughter went out to the woodshed and returned with the axe.

"Now chop off my head, my own true love. Remember the promise you made to me, when fetching your water down at the well," croaked the frog to the daughter.

Trembling, the girl turned to the frog, who stretched out his neck obligingly. She raised the axe high, just as she did when chopping wood for the fire, and brought it down on to the frog's neck. When she had done the deed, the girl looked away for a moment, scared to see the dead creature and its severed head. But when she heard her mother's shout of surprise she looked back quickly. And there stood the finest, most handsome young prince that either of them had ever seen.

"It was me you promised to marry," smiled the prince.

And the poor widow's daughter and the handsome prince *did* marry, and they lived in happiness for rest of their lives.

MINNIE AND MATTIE

Minnie and Mattie
  And fat little May,
Out in the country,
  Spending a day.

Such a bright day,
  With the sun glowing,
And the trees half in leaf,
  And the grass growing.

Pinky white pigling
  Squeals through his snout,
Woolly white lambkin
  Frisks all about.

Cluck! cluck! the nursing hen
  Summons her folk,—
Ducklings all downy soft,
  Yellow as yolk.

Cluck! cluck! the mother hen
  Summons her chickens
To peck the dainty bits
  Found in her pickings.

Minnie and Mattie
  And May carry posies,
Half of sweet violets,
  Half of primroses.

Give the sun time enough,
　Glowing and glowing,
He'll rouse the roses
　And bring them blowing.

Don't wait for roses
　Losing today,
O Minnie, Mattie,
　And wise little May.

Violets and primroses
　Blossom to-day
For Minnie and Mattie
　And fat little May.

CHRISTINA ROSSETTI

A THORN

I went to the wood and got it;
I sat me down and looked at it;
The more I looked at it the less I liked it;
And I brought it home because I couldn't help it.

TEETH

Thirty white horses upon a red hill,
Now they tramp, now they champ,
    now they stand still.

A STAR

I have a little sister, they call her Peep, Peep;
She wades the waters deep, deep, deep;
She climbs the mountains high, high, high;
Poor little creature she has but one eye.

OVER THE HILLS AND FAR AWAY

When I was young and had no sense
I bought a fiddle for eighteenpence,
And the only tune that I could play
Was "Over the Hills and Far Away".

HEY, DIDDLE, DIDDLE

Hey, diddle, diddle, the cat and the fiddle,
The cow jumped over the moon;
The little dog laughed to see such sport,
And the dish ran away with the spoon!

POLLY, PUT THE KETTLE ON

Polly, put the kettle on,
Polly, put the kettle on,
Polly, put the kettle on,
   And we'll all have tea.

Sukey, take it off again,
Sukey, take it off again,
Sukey, take it off again,
   They're all gone away.

A PRETTY LITTLE GIRL

A pretty little girl in a round-eared cap
I met in the streets the other day;
    She gave me such a thump,
    That my heart it went bump;
I thought I should have fainted away!
I thought I should have fainted away!

A SWARM OF BEES IN MAY

A swarm of bees in May
Is worth a load of hay;
A swarm of bees in June
Is worth a silver spoon;
A swarm of bees in July
Is not worth a fly.

INCEY WINCEY SPIDER

Incey Wincey spider
   Climbing up the spout;
Down came the rain
   And washed the spider out:
Out came the sunshine
   And dried up all the rain;
Incey Wincey spider
   Climbing up again.

OLIVER TWIST

Oliver Twist
You can't do this,
So what's the use
Of trying?
Touch your toe,
Touch your knee,
Clap your hands,
Away we go.

A SAILOR WENT TO SEA

A sailor went to sea, sea, sea,
To see what he could see, see, see,
But all that he could see, see, see,
Was the bottom of the deep blue sea, sea, sea.

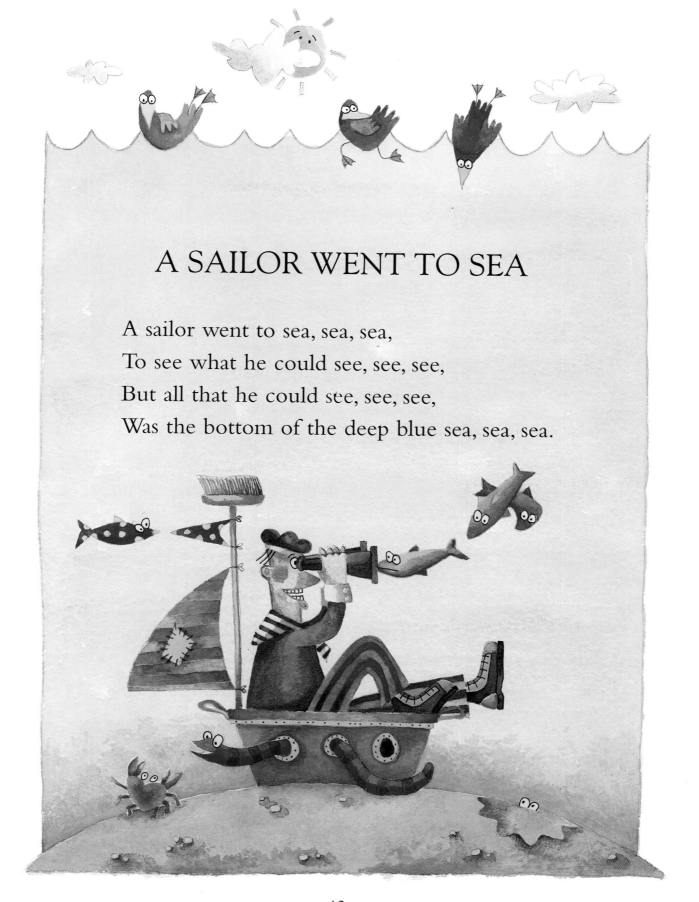

43

THE MISSING KETTLE

There was a woman who lived on the island of Sanntraigh, and she had only a kettle to hang over the fire to boil her water and cook her food. Every day one of the fairy folk would come to take the kettle. She would slip into the house quietly without saying a word, and grab hold of the kettle handle.

Each time this happened, the kettle handle made a clanking noise and the woman looked up and recited this rhyme:

> A smith is able to make
> Cold iron hot with coal.
> The due of a kettle is bones,
> And to bring it back again whole.

Then the fairy would fly away with the kettle and the woman would not see it again until later in the day, when the fairy brought it back, filled with flesh and bones.

There came at last a day when the woman had to leave home and go on the ferry across to the mainland. She turned to her husband, who was making a rope of heather to keep the thatch on the roof. "Will you say the rhyme that I say when the fairy comes for the kettle?" Her husband said that he would recite the rhyme just as she did, and went back to his work.

After the woman had left to catch the boat, the fairy arrived as usual, and the husband saw her come to the door. When he saw her he started to feel afraid, for unlike his wife he had had no contact with the little people. "If I lock the cottage door," he reasoned to himself, "she will go away and leave the kettle, and it will be just as if she had never come." So the husband locked the door and did not open it when the fairy tried to come in.

But instead of going away, the fairy flew up to the hole in the roof where the smoke from the fire escaped, and before the husband knew what was happening, the creature had made the kettle jump right up and out of the hole. The fairy made away with the kettle before he knew what to do.

When his wife returned that evening, there was no kettle to be seen.

"What have you done with my kettle?" asked the woman.

"I've done nothing with it," said the husband. "But I took fright when the fairy came, closed the door to her, she took the kettle through the roof, and now it is gone."

"You pathetic wretch! Can't you even mind the kettle when I go out for the day?"

The husband tried to tell his wife that the fairy might return the kettle the next day, but the woman would hear nothing of it. Off she went straight away to the knoll where the fairies lived, to see if she could get back the kettle herself.

It was quite dark when she reached the fairies' knoll. The hillside opened to her and when she went in she saw only an old fairy sitting in the corner. The woman supposed that the others were out at their nightly mischief. Soon she found her kettle, and noticed that it still contained the remains of the food the little people had cooked in it.

She picked up the kettle and ran back down the lane, when she heard the sound of dogs chasing her. The old fairy must have let them loose. Thinking quickly, she took out some of the food from the kettle, threw it to the dogs, and hurried on.

This slowed down the dogs, and when they began to catch her up again, she threw down more food. Finally, when she got near her own gate, she poured out the rest of the food, hoping that the dogs would not come into her own house. Then she ran inside and closed the door.

Every day after that the woman watched for the fairy coming to take her kettle. But the little creature never came again.

WHEN THAT I WAS AND A LITTLE TINY BOY

When that I was and a little tiny boy,
  With hey, ho, the wind and the rain;
A foolish thing was but a toy,
  For the rain it raineth every day.

But when I came to man's estate,
  With hey, ho, the wind and the rain;
'Gainst knaves and thieves men shut their gate,
  For the rain it raineth every day.

A great while ago the world begun,
  With hey, ho, the wind and the rain;
But that's all one, our play is done,
  And we'll strive to please you every day.

WILLIAM SHAKESPEARE

I EAT MY PEAS WITH HONEY

I eat my peas with honey,
I've done it all my life,
It makes the peas taste funny,
But it keeps them on my knife.

ANONYMOUS
AMERICAN

LADY MOON

Lady Moon, Lady Moon, where are you roving?
    Over the sea.
Lady Moon, Lady Moon, whom are you loving?
    All that love me.

Are you not tired with rolling, and never
    Resting to sleep?
Why look so pale, and so sad, as for ever
    Wishing to weep?

Ask me not this, little child, if you love me;
    You are too bold;
I must obey my dear Father above me,
    And do as I'm told.

Lady Moon, Lady Moon, where are you roving?
    Over the sea.
Lady Moon, Lady Moon, whom are you loving?
    All that love me.

RICHARD MONCKTON MILNES, LORD HOUGHTON

THE MOON

The moon has a face like the clock in the hall;
She shines on thieves on the garden wall,
On streets and fields and harbour quays,
And birdies asleep in the forks of the trees.

The squalling cat and the squeaking mouse,
The howling dog by the door of the house,
The bat that lies in bed at noon,
All love to be out by the light of the moon.

But all of the things that belong to the day
Cuddle to sleep to be out of her way;
And flowers and children close their eyes
Till up in the morning the sun shall arise.

ROBERT LOUIS STEVENSON

51

IF ALL THE WORLD WAS APPLE-PIE

If all the world was apple-pie,
  And all the sea was ink,
And all the trees were bread and cheese,
  What should we have for drink?

FOR WANT OF A NAIL

For want of a nail, the shoe was lost;
For want of the shoe, the horse was lost;
For want of the horse, the rider was lost;
For want of the rider, the battle was lost;
For want of the battle, the kingdom was lost;
And all from the want of a horseshoe nail.

53

HUMPTY DUMPTY

Humpty Dumpty sat on a wall,
Humpty Dumpty had a great fall;
All the king's horses and all the king's men
Couldn't put Humpty together again.

TWEEDLE-DUM AND TWEEDLE-

Tweedle-dum and Tweedle-dee
  Agreed to have a battle,
For Tweedle-dum said Tweedle-dee
  Had spoiled his nice new rattle.
Just then flew down a monstrous crow,
  As big as a tar-barrel,
Which frightened both the heroes so,
  They quite forgot their quarrel.

MY GRANDMOTHER SENT ME

My grandmother sent me a new-fashioned three cornered cambric country cut handkerchief. Not an old-fashioned three cornered cambric country cut handkerchief, but a new-fashioned three cornered cambric country cut handkerchief.

ROBERT ROWLEY

Robert Rowley rolled a round roll round,
A round roll Robert Rowley rolled round;
Where rolled the round roll Robert Rowley
    rolled round?

SWAN SWAM OVER THE SEA

Swan swam over the sea—
Swim, swan, swim,
Swan swam back again,
Well swum swan.

HEY, DOROLOT, DOROLOT!

Hey, dorolot, dorolot!
Hey, dorolay, dorolay!
Hey, my bonny boat, bonny boat,
Hey, drag away, drag away!

RUB-A-DUB DUB

Rub-a-dub dub,
Three men in a tub,
And who do you think they be?
The butcher, the baker,
The candle-stick maker,
And they all jumped out of a rotten potato.

DOCTOR FOSTER WENT TO GLOUCESTER

Doctor Foster went to Gloucester,
  In a shower of rain;
He stepped in a puddle, up to his middle,
  And never went there again.

I REMEMBER, I REMEMBER

I remember, I remember
The house where I was born,
The little window where the sun
Came peeping in at morn;
He never came a wink too soon
Nor brought too long a day;
But now, I often wish the night
Had borne my breath away.

I remember, I remember
The roses, red and white,
The violets, and the lily-cups—
Those flowers made of light!
The lilacs where the robin built,
And where my brother set
The laburnum on his birthday,—
The tree is living yet!

I remember, I remember
Where I was used to swing,
And thought the air must rush as fresh
To swallows on the wing;
My spirit flew in feathers then
That is so heavy now,
And summer pools could hardly cool
The fever on my brow.

I remember, I remember
The fir trees dark and high;
I used to think their slender tops
Were close against the sky:
It was a childish ignorance,
But now 'tis little joy
To know I'm farther off from Heaven
Than when I was a boy.

THOMAS HOOD

MY SHADOW

I have a little shadow that goes in and out with me,
And what can be the use of him is more than I can see.
He is very, very like me from the heels up to the head;
And I see him jump before me,
   when I jump into my bed.

The funniest thing about him is the way he likes to grow—
Not at all like proper children, which is always very slow;
For he sometimes shoots up taller like an india-rubber ball,
And he sometimes gets so little that
   there's none of him at all.

He hasn't got a notion of how children ought to play,

And can only make a fool of me in every sort of way.

He stays so close beside me, he's a coward you can see;

I'd think shame to stick to nursie

  as that shadow sticks to me!

One morning, very early, before the sun was up,

I rose and found the shining dew on every buttercup;

But my lazy little shadow, like an arrant sleepyhead,

Had stayed at home behind me and was

  fast asleep in bed.

ROBERT LOUIS STEVENSON

THE DAYS ARE CLEAR

The days are clear,
    Day after day,
When April's here
    That leads to May,
And June
Must follow soon:
    Stay, June, stay!—
If only we could stop the moon
And June!

CHRISTINA ROSETTI

AUTUMN FIRES

In the other gardens
   And all up the vale,
From the autumn bonfires
   See the smoke trail!

Pleasant summer over
   And all the summer flowers,
The red fire blazes,
   The grey smoke towers.

Sing a song of seasons!
   Something bright in all!
Flowers in the summer,
   Fires in the fall!

ROBERT LOUIS STEVENSON

THE HUMBLE-BEE

Two young men were out walking one summer's day and stopped by a tiny stream next to an old ruined house. They were admiring the place, and noticed how the stream turned into a miniature waterfall crossed by narrow blades of grass. One of the men was tired from the walk and the afternoon heat and sat down by the stream. Soon he was fast asleep, and the other sat quietly, watching the view.

Suddenly, a tiny creature, about the size of a humble-bee, flew out of the sleeper's mouth. It landed by the stream and crossed it by walking over some grass stalks which hung over the water at its narrowest point. The creature then approached the ruin and disappeared into one of the cracks in the wall.

The man who saw all this was shocked and decided to wake his friend to see if he was all right. As he shook his companion awake, he was astonished to see the tiny creature emerge from the ruin, fly across the stream and re-enter the sleeper's mouth, just as the young man was waking.

"What's the matter? Are you ill?" asked the watcher.

"I am well," replied the sleeper. "You have just interrupted the most wonderful dream, and I wish you had not woken me

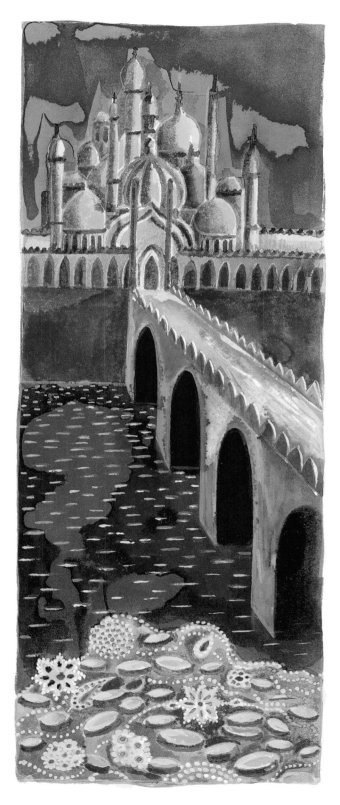

with your shaking. I dreamed that I walked through a vast grassy plain and came to a wide river. I wanted to cross the river to see what was on the other side, and I found a place near a great waterfall where there was a bridge made of silver. I walked over the bridge and on the far bank was a beautiful palace built of stone. When I looked in, the chambers of the palace contained great mounds of gold and jewels. I was looking at all these fine things, wondering at the wealth of the person who left them there, and deciding which I would bring away with me. Then suddenly you woke me, and I could bring away none of the riches."

THE WIND

Who has seen the wind?
  Neither I nor you;
But when the leaves hang trembling
  The wind is passing through.

Who has seen the wind?
  Neither you nor I;
But when the trees bow down their heads
  The wind is passing by.

CHRISTINA ROSSETTI

FROM A RAILWAY CARRIAGE

Faster than fairies, faster than witches,
Bridges and houses, hedges and ditches;
And charging along like troops in a battle,
All through the meadows the horses and cattle:
All of the sights of the hill and the plain
Fly as thick as driving rain;
And ever again, in the wink of an eye,
Painted stations whistle by.

Here is a child who clambers and scrambles,
All by himself and gathering brambles;
Here is a tramp who stands and gazes;
And there is the green for stringing the daisies!
Here is a cart run away in the road
Lumping along with man and load;
And here is a mill, and there is a river:
Each a glimpse and gone for ever!

ROBERT LOUIS STEVENSON

FROM WIBBLETON TO WOBBLETON

From Wibbleton to Wobbleton
  is fifteen miles,
From Wobbleton to Wibbleton
  is fifteen miles,
From Wibbleton to Wobbleton,
From Wobbleton to Wibbleton,
From Wibbleton to Wobbleton
  is fifteen miles.

SEE-SAW, SACRADOWN

See–saw, Sacradown,
Which is the way to London Town?
One foot up and one foot down,
That's the way to London Town.

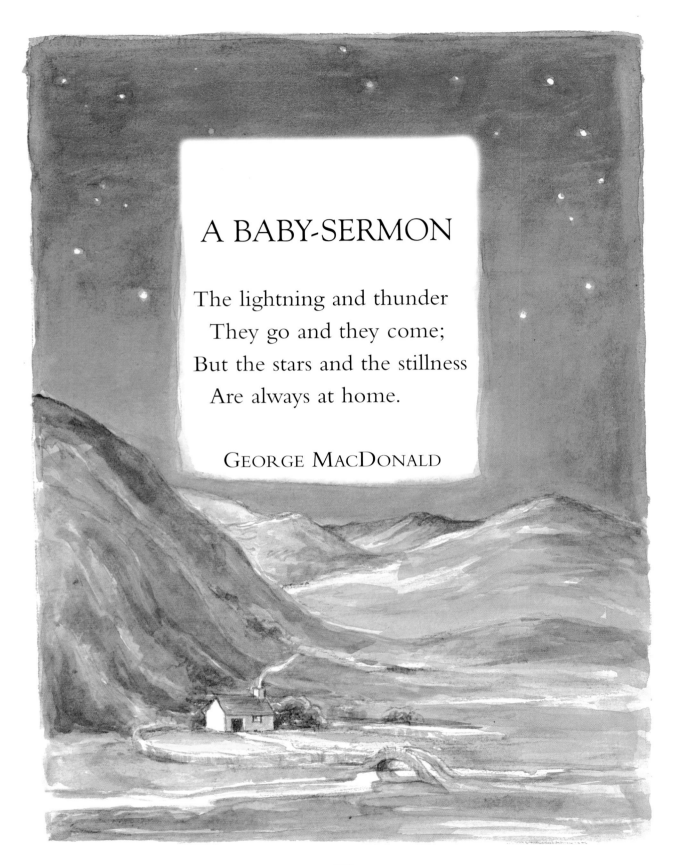

A BABY-SERMON

The lightning and thunder
They go and they come;
But the stars and the stillness
Are always at home.

GEORGE MACDONALD

WAGTAIL AND BABY

A baby watched a ford, whereto
 A wagtail came for drinking;
A blaring bull went wading through,
 The wagtail showed no shrinking.

A stallion splashed his way across,
 The birdie nearly sinking;
He gave his plumes a twitch and toss,
 And held his own unblinking.

Next saw the baby round the spot
 A mongrel slowing slinking;
The wagtail gazed, but faltered not
 In dip and sip and prinking.

A perfect gentleman then neared;
 The wagtail, in a winking,
With terror rose and disappeared;
 The baby fell a-thinking.

THOMAS HARDY

73

SOLOMON GRUNDY

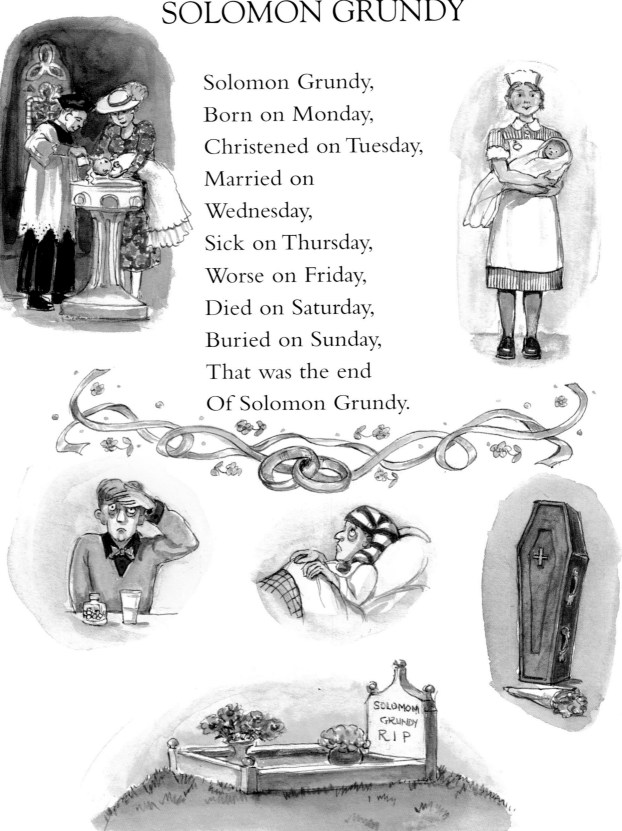

Solomon Grundy,
Born on Monday,
Christened on Tuesday,
Married on
Wednesday,
Sick on Thursday,
Worse on Friday,
Died on Saturday,
Buried on Sunday,
That was the end
Of Solomon Grundy.

OLD KING COLE

Old King Cole
Was a merry old soul,
And a merry old soul was he;
He called for his pipe,
And he called for his bowl,
And he called for his fiddlers three.
Every fiddler had a fine fiddle,
And a very fine fiddle had he;
Twee tweedle dee, tweedle dee, went the fiddlers,
    Very merry men are we;
    Oh there's none so rare
    As can compare
With King Cole and his fiddlers three.

THE SUGAR-PLUM TREE

Have you ever heard of the Sugar-Plum Tree?
　'Tis a marvel of great renown!
It blooms on the shore of the Lollipop sea
　In the garden of Shut-Eye Town:
The fruit that it bears is so wondrously sweet
　(As those who have tasted it say)
That good little children have only to eat
　Of that fruit to be happy next day.

When you've got to the tree, you would have a hard time
　To capture the fruit which I sing;
The tree is so tall that no person could climb
　To the boughs where the sugar-plums swing.
But up in that tree sits a chocolate cat,
　And a gingerbread dog prowls below—
And this is the way you contrive to get at
　Those sugar-plums tempting you so:

You say but the word to that gingerbread dog
  And he barks with such terrible zest
That the chocolate cat is at once all agog,
  As her swelling proportions attest.
And the chocolate cat goes cavorting around
  From this leafy limb unto that,
And the sugar-plums tumble, of course, to the ground—
  Hurrah for that chocolate cat!

There are marshmallows, gumdrops, and peppermint canes,
  With striplings of scarlet or gold,
And you carry away of the treasure that rains
  As much as your apron can hold!
So come, little child, cuddle closer to me
  In your dainty white nightcap and gown,
And I'll rock you away to that Sugar-Plum Tree
  In the garden of Shut-Eye Town.

EUGENE FIELD

LIE A-BED

Lie a-bed,
Sleepy head,
Shut up eyes, bo-peep;
Till day-break
Never wake:—
Baby, sleep.

Christina Rossetti

HAPPY THOUGHT

The world is so full of a number of things,
I'm sure we should all be as happy as kings.

R OBERT L OUIS S TEVENSON

THE MAIDEN FROM THE LAKE

There was once a shepherd who lived in Myddvai, by the mountains of Caermarthen. A great lake was near his pastures, and one day he was watching his sheep near its shores when he saw three beautiful maidens rise from the waters. The young women came to the shore, shook the water from their hair, and walked around among the sheep.

The shepherd was overcome by the beauty of the maiden who came nearest to him, and he offered her some bread from his pack. The girl took the bread, tried a little, and said to the shepherd, "Your bread's too hard. You won't catch me." Then she ran back to the lake with the others.

The shepherd wondered whether he would see the maidens again, but just in case, on the next day, he brought some bread that was not so well baked. To his delight, the maidens appeared again, and he offered the softer bread. But this time the girl said, "Your bread's not baked. You won't catch me." Once more, she returned to the water.

On the third day, the shepherd waited for the young woman. When she came, he offered her some bread that had been floating on the water. This she liked, and the couple talked for a long while. Finally, the maiden agreed to marry the shepherd, but gave this warning: she would be a good wife to him, as good as any ordinary Welsh woman, unless he struck her three times without reason. The shepherd vowed that he would never do this, and the couple were soon married.

The shepherd and his bride were happy, and in time had three fine sons. It happened that they were going to christen one of the children when the wife said that it was too far to walk to church.

"Then go and get the horses," said the shepherd, "and we will ride all the way."

"While I get the horses, will you fetch my gloves from the house?" asked his wife.

But when the shepherd returned with the gloves he found that she had not fetched the horses, and he tapped her gently on the shoulder to remind her.

"That's one strike," said his wife.

A little while later, the pair were at a friend's wedding. The shepherd found his wife crying and again he tapped her on the shoulder as he asked her what was wrong.

"Trouble is coming for you," she replied. "That is the second time you have struck me without reason. Take care to avoid the third time."

From then on, the shepherd was careful not so much as to tap his wife, until one day the couple were at a funeral. All of a sudden, the wife began to laugh loudly. The shepherd was amazed. He could not understand why anyone should laugh at such a sad time, so, touching her rather roughly, he said, "Wife, why are you laughing when all around you are sad?"

"I am laughing because people who die leave their troubles behind them. But your troubles have just begun. You have struck me for a third time. Now I must make an end to our marriage and bid you farewell."

The shepherd knew that the time had come for his wife to leave him, and he was sad to the bottom of his heart. But he was still more surprised when he heard his wife calling all the cattle around her, bidding them follow her to her home beneath the waters of the lake. He saw all his cattle, even a black calf that had recently been slaughtered and a team of oxen that were ploughing a field, get up and follow her away. The oxen even took their plough with them, cutting a deep furrow all the way to the shore.

The mark left by the plough can still be seen running across the pastures by the lake. But the lady has only been seen once more. When her sons had grown up, she returned to visit them. She gave them miraculous gifts of healing. And ever since, the Doctors of Myddvai have been famous throughout the land of Wales.

83

HUSH, LITTLE BABY

Hush, little baby, don't say a word,
Papa's going to buy you a mocking bird.

If the mocking bird won't sing,
Papa's going to buy you a diamond ring.

If the diamond ring turn to brass,
Papa's going to buy you a looking-glass.

If the looking-glass gets broke,
Papa's going to buy you a billy-goat.

If that billy-goat runs away,
Papa's going to buy you another today.

ANONYMOUS
AMERICAN

THE MOUSE'S LULLABY

Oh, rock-a-by, baby mouse, rock-a-by, so!
When baby's asleep to the baker's I'll go,
And while he's not looking I'll pop from a hole,
And bring to my baby a fresh penny roll.

PALMER COX

OLD JOE BROWN

Old Joe Brown, he had a wife,
　　She was all of eight feet tall.
She slept with her head in the kitchen,
　　And her feet stuck out in the hall.

JEREMIAH

Jeremiah
Jumped in the fire.
Fire was so hot
He jumped in the pot.
Pot was so little
He jumped in the kettle.
Kettle was so black
He jumped in the crack.
Crack was so high
He jumped in the sky.
Sky was so blue
He jumped in a canoe.
Canoe was so deep
He jumped in the creek.
Creek was so shallow
He jumped in the tallow.
Tallow was so soft
He jumped in the loft.
Loft was so rotten
He jumped in the cotton.
Cotton was so white
He jumped all night.

I HAD A LITTLE NUT TREE

I had a little nut tree, nothing would it bear,
But a silver nutmeg, and a golden pear;
The King of Spain's daughter came to visit me,
And all for the sake of my little nut tree.
I skipped over water, I danced over sea,
And all the birds of the air couldn't catch me.

HOW MANY MILES TO BABYLON?

How many miles to Babylon?—
  Threescore and ten.
Can I get there by candlelight?—
  Aye, and back again!

89

THE BUTTERFLY'S BALL

Come take up your hats, and away let us haste,
To the Butterfly's Ball, and the Grasshopper's Feast.
The trumpeter Gadfly has summoned the crew,
And the revels are now only waiting for you.

On the smooth-shaven grass by the side of a wood,
Beneath a broad oak which for ages has stood,
See the children of earth and the tenants of air,
For an evening's amusement together repair.

And there came the Beetle, so blind and so black,
Who carried the Emmet, his friend, on his back.
And there came the Gnat, and the Dragonfly too,
And all their relations, green, orange, and blue.

And there came the Moth, with her plumage of down,
And the Hornet, with jacket of yellow and brown;
Who with him the Wasp, his companion, did bring,
But they promised that evening, to lay by their sting.

Then the sly little Dormouse crept out of his hole,
And led to the feast his blind cousin the Mole.
And the Snail, with his horns peeping out of his shell,
Came, fatigued with the distance, the length of an ell.

A mushroom their table, and on it was laid
A water-dock leaf, which a tablecloth made.
The viands were various, to each of their taste,
And the Bee brought the honey to sweeten the feast.

With steps most majestic the Snail did advance,
And he promised the gazers a minuet to dance;
But they all laughed so loud that he drew in his head,
And went in his own little chamber to bed.

Then, as evening gave way to the shadows of night,
Their watchman, the Glow-worm, came out with his light.
So home let us hasten, while yet we can see;
For no watchman is waiting for you and for me.

WILLIAM ROSCOE

91

THE STORY OF THE LITTLE BIRD

Once long ago in a monastery in Ireland there lived a holy man. He was walking one day in the garden of his monastery, when he decided to kneel down and pray, to give thanks to God for the beauty of all the flowers and plants and herbs around him. As he did so, he heard a small bird singing, and never before had he heard any song as sweet. When his prayers, were finished, the monk stood up and listened to the bird, and when the creature flew away from the garden, singing as it went, he followed it.

In a while they came to a small grove of trees outside the monastery grounds, and there the bird continued its song. As the bird hopped from tree to tree, still singing all the while, the monk carried on following the little creature, until they had gone a great distance. The more the bird sang, the more the monk was enchanted by the music it made.

Eventually, the two had travelled far away from the monastery, and the monk realised that it would soon be night-time. So reluctantly, he left the bird behind and retraced his steps, arriving back home as the sun was going down in the west. As the sun set, it lit up the sky with all the colours of the rainbow, and the monk thought that the sight was almost as beautiful and heavenly as the song of the little bird he had been listening to all afternoon long.

But the glorious sunset was not the only sight that surprised the monk. As he entered the abbey gates, everything around him seemed changed from before. In the garden grew different plants, in the courtyard the brothers had different faces, and even the abbey buildings seemed to have altered. He knew he was in the right place, yet how could all these changes have taken place in a single afternoon?

The holy man walked across the courtyard and greeted the

first monk he saw. "Brother, how is it that our abbey has changed so much since this morning? There are fresh plants in the garden, new faces amongst the brothers, and even the stones of the church seem different."

The second monk looked at the holy man carefully. "Why do you ask these questions, brother? There have been no changes. Our church and gardens have not altered since morning, and we have no new brothers here – except for yourself, for though you wear the habit of our order, I have not seen you before." And the two monks looked at each other in wonder. Neither could understand what had happened.

When he saw that the

brother was puzzled, the holy man started to tell his story. He told his companion how he had gone to walk in the monastery garden, how he had heard the little bird, and how he had followed the creature far into the countryside to listen to its song.

As the holy man spoke, the expression on the second monk's face turned from puzzlement to surprise. He said, "There is a story in our order about a brother like you who went missing one day after a bird was heard singing. He never returned to the abbey, and no one knew what befell him, and all this happened two hundred years ago."

The holy man looked at his companion and replied, "That is indeed my story. The time of my death has finally arrived. Praised be the Lord for his mercies to me." And the holy man begged the second monk to take his confession and give him absolution, for the hour of his death was near. All this was done, the holy man died before midnight, and he was buried with great solemnity in the abbey church.

Ever since, the monks of the abbey have told this story. They say that the little bird was an angel of the Lord, and that this was God's way of taking the soul of a man who was known for his holiness and his love of the beauties of nature.

FOLLOW MY BANGALOREY MAN

Follow my Bangalorey Man,
Follow my Bangalorey Man;
I'll do all that ever I can
To follow my Bangalorey Man.
We'll borrow a horse, and steal a gig,
And round the world we'll do a jig,
And I'll do all that ever I can
To follow my Bangalorey Man!

ANNA MARIA

Anna Maria she sat on the fire;
The fire was too hot, she sat on the pot;
The pot was too round, she sat on the ground;
The ground was too flat, she sat on the cat;
The cat ran away with Maria on her back.

GO TO BED, TOM

Go to bed, Tom,
Go to bed, Tom,
Tired or not, Tom,
Go to bed, Tom.

HIGGLEDY PIGGLEDY

Higgledy piggledy,
  Here we lie,
Picked and plucked,
  And put in a pie!

WEE WILLIE WINKIE

Wee Willie Winkie runs through the town,
Up-stairs and down-stairs in his nightgown,
Peeping through the keyhole, crying through the lock,
"Are the children in their beds, it's past eight o'clock?"

PETER, PETER, PUMPKIN EATER

Peter, Peter, pumpkin eater,
Had a wife and couldn't keep her;
He put her in a pumpkin shell
And there he kept her very well.

Peter, Peter, pumpkin eater,
Had another and didn't love her;
Peter learned to read and spell,
And then he loved her very well.

SIMPLE SIMON

Simple Simon met a pieman
   Going to the fair;
Said Simple Simon to the pieman,
   "Let me taste your ware."

Said the pieman to Simple Simon,
   "Show me first your penny";
Said Simple Simon to the pieman,
   "Indeed I have not any."

GIRLS AND BOYS COME OUT TO PLAY

Girls and boys, come out to play;
The moon doth shine as bright as day;
Leave your supper, and leave your sleep,
And come with your playfellows into the street.
Come with a whoop, come with a call,
Come with a good will or not at all.
Up the ladder and down the wall,
A halfpenny roll will serve us all.
You find milk, and I'll find flour,
And we'll have a pudding in half-an-hour.

GEORGIE, PORGIE

Georgie, Porgie, pudding and pie,
Kissed the girls and made them cry;
When the boys came out to play
Georgie Porgie ran away.

I SCREAM

I scream, you scream,
We all scream for ice cream!

SNEEZE ON MONDAY

Sneeze on Monday, sneeze for danger;
Sneeze on Tuesday, kiss a stranger;
Sneeze on Wednesday, get a letter;
Sneeze on Thursday, something better;
Sneeze on Friday, sneeze for sorrow;
Sneeze on Saturday, see your sweetheart
   tomorrow.

SEE A PIN AND PICK IT UP

See a pin and pick it up,
All the day you'll have good luck;
See a pin and let it lay,
Bad luck you'll have all the day!

RAIN, RAIN, GO AWAY

Rain, rain, go away,
Come again another day.

THE SWING

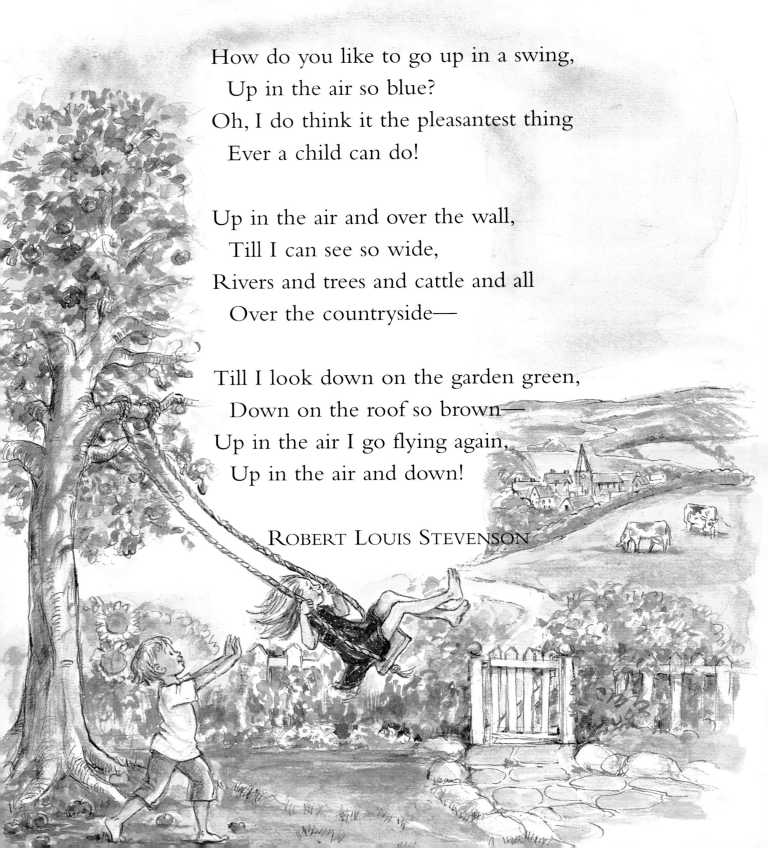

How do you like to go up in a swing,
   Up in the air so blue?
Oh, I do think it the pleasantest thing
   Ever a child can do!

Up in the air and over the wall,
   Till I can see so wide,
Rivers and trees and cattle and all
   Over the countryside—

Till I look down on the garden green,
   Down on the roof so brown—
Up in the air I go flying again,
   Up in the air and down!

ROBERT LOUIS STEVENSON

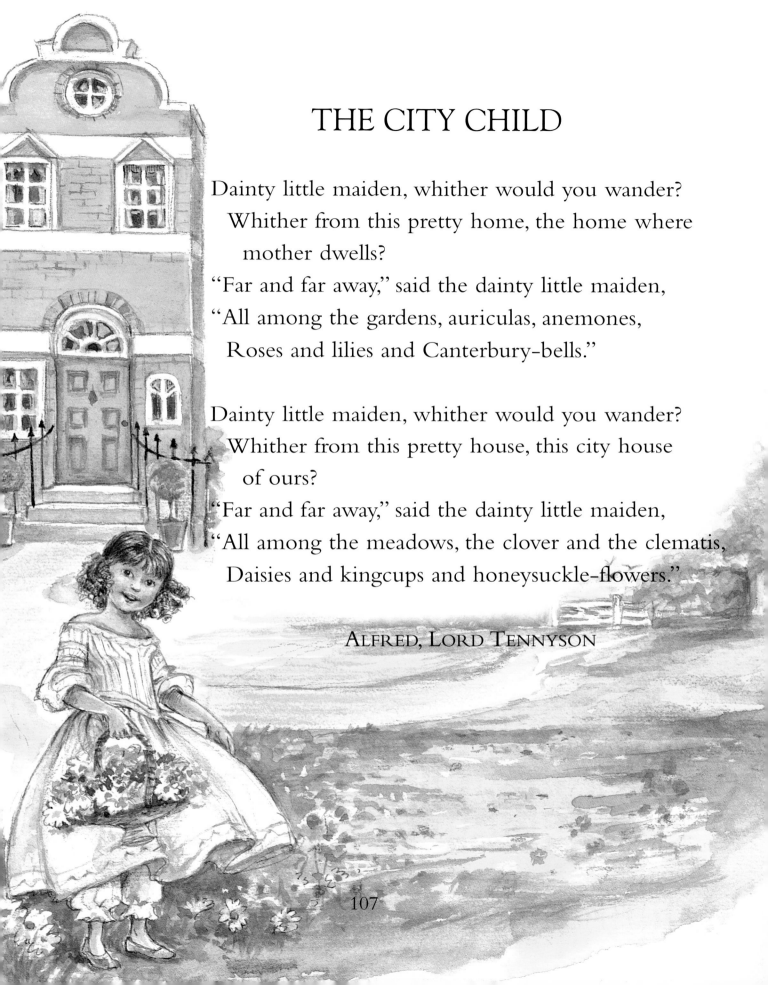

THE CITY CHILD

Dainty little maiden, whither would you wander?
  Whither from this pretty home, the home where
    mother dwells?
"Far and far away," said the dainty little maiden,
"All among the gardens, auriculas, anemones,
  Roses and lilies and Canterbury-bells."

Dainty little maiden, whither would you wander?
  Whither from this pretty house, this city house
    of ours?
"Far and far away," said the dainty little maiden,
"All among the meadows, the clover and the clematis,
  Daisies and kingcups and honeysuckle-flowers."

ALFRED, LORD TENNYSON

THREE WISE MEN OF GOTHAM

Three wise men of Gotham
Went to sea in a bowl:
And if the bowl had been stronger,
My song would have been longer.

JACKANORY

I'll tell you a story
Of Jackanory,
And now my story's begun;
I'll tell you another
Of Jack his brother,
And now my story's done.

ONCE I SAW A LITTLE BIRD

Once I saw a little bird
Come hop, hop, hop;
So I cried, "Little bird,
Will you stop, stop, stop?"
And was going to the window,
To say, "How do you do?"
But he shook his little tail,
And far away he flew.

JAY-BIRD

Jay-bird, jay-bird, settin' on a rail,
Pickin' his teeth with the end of his tail;
Mulberry leaves and calico sleeves—
All school teachers are hard to please.

BIRDS OF A FEATHER

Birds of a feather flock together
And so will pigs and swine;
Rats and mice shall have their choice,
And so shall I have mine.

ROBIN AND RICHARD

Robin and Richard were two pretty men;
They laid in bed till the clock struck ten;
Then up starts Robin and looks at the sky,
Oh! brother Richard, the sun's very high:

The bull's in the barn threshing the corn,
The cock's on the dunghill blowing his horn,
The cat's at the fire frying of fish,
The dog's in the pantry breaking his dish.

LITTLE TOMMY TITTLEMOUSE

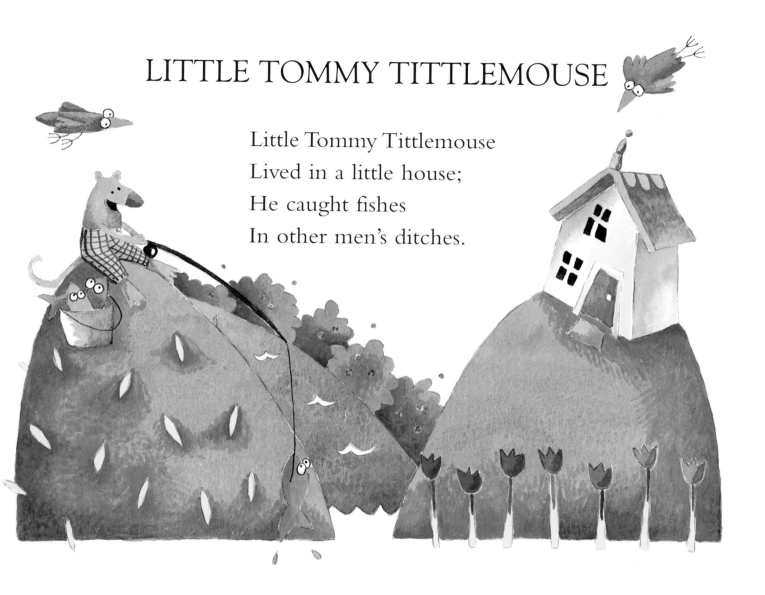

Little Tommy Tittlemouse
Lived in a little house;
He caught fishes
In other men's ditches.

SEE-SAW, MARGERY DAW

See-saw, Margery Daw,
  Jack shall have a new master;
He shall have but a penny a day,
  Because he can't work any faster.

113

HURT NO LIVING THING

Hurt no living thing,
  Ladybird nor butterfly,
Nor moth with dusty wing,
Nor cricket chirping cheerily,
Nor grasshopper, so light of leap,
  Nor dancing gnat,
  Nor beetle fat,
Nor harmless worms that creep.

CHRISTINA ROSSETTI

114

THE COW

The friendly cow all red and white,
  I love with all my heart:
She gives me cream with all her might,
  To eat with apple-tart.

She wanders lowing here and there,
  And yet she cannot stray,
All in the pleasant open air,
  The pleasant light of day;

And blown by all the winds that pass
  And wet with all the showers,
She walks among the meadow grass
  And eats the meadow flowers.

ROBERT LOUIS STEVENSON

HUSH-A-BYE, BABY

Hush-a-bye, baby, on the tree top,
When the wind blows the cradle will rock;
When the bough breaks the cradle will fall,
Down will come baby, cradle and all.

ALL THE PRETTY LITTLE HORSES

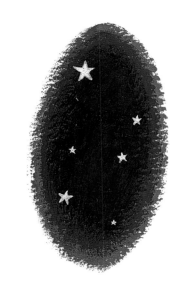

Hush–a–bye, don't you cry,
Go to sleepy little baby.
When you wake
You shall have
All the pretty little horses.
Blacks and bays,
Dapples and greys,
Coach and six white horses.

Hush–a–bye, don't you cry,
Go to sleepy little baby.
When you wake
You shall have cake
And all the pretty little horses.

LEG OVER LEG

Leg over leg,
    As the dog went to Dover;
When he came to a stile,
    Jump he went over.

MICHAEL FINNEGAN

There was an old man called Michael Finnegan
He grew whiskers on his chinnegan
The wind came out and blew them in again
Poor old Michael Finnegan. *Begin again...*

118

RIDE A COCK-HORSE

Ride a cock-horse to Banbury Cross,
  To see a fine lady ride on a white horse,
Rings on her fingers and bells on her toes,
  She shall have music wherever she goes.

I AM A GOLD LOCK

FOR TWO VOICES

I am a gold lock.
I am a gold key.
I am a silver lock.
I am a silver key.
I am a brass lock.
I am a brass key.
I am a lead lock.
I am a lead key.
I am a monk lock.
I am a monk key!

I WENT UP ONE PAIR OF STAIRS

FOR TWO VOICES

I went up one pair of stairs.
Just like me.
I went up two pair of stairs.
Just like me.
I went into a room.
Just like me.
I looked out of a window.
Just like me.
And there I saw a monkey.
Just like me.

THE DUEL

The gingham dog and the calico cat
    Side by side on the table sat;
'Twas half-past twelve, and (what do you think!)
Nor one nor t'other had slept a wink!
    The old Dutch clock and the Chinese plate
    Appeared to know as sure as fate
There was going to be a terrible spat.
    (I wasn't there; I simply state
    What was told to me by the Chinese plate!)

The gingham dog went "Bow-wow-wow!
And the calico cat replied "mee-ow!"
The air was littered, an hour or so,
With bits of gingham and calico,
    While the old Dutch clock in the chimney-place
    Up with its hands before its face,
For it always dreaded a family row!
    (Now mind: I'm only telling you
    What the old Dutch clock declares is true!)

Mee-ow

Bow-
wow-
wow

The Chinese plate looked very blue,
And wailed, "Oh, dear! what shall we do?"
But the gingham dog and the calico cat
Wallowed this way and tumbled that,
 Employing every tooth and claw
 In the awfullest way you ever saw—
And, oh! how the gingham and calico flew!
 (Don't fancy I exaggerate!
 I got my news from the Chinese plate!)

Next morning, where the two had sat,
They found no trace of dog or cat;
And some folks think unto this day
That burglars stole that pair away!
 But the truth about the cat and pup
 Is this: they ate each other up!
Now what do you really think of that!
 (The old Dutch clock it told me so,
 And that is how I came to know.)

EUGENE FIELD

SONG OF THE SKY LOOM

O our Mother the Earth, O our Father the Sky,
Your children are we, and with tired backs
We bring you the gifts that you love.
Then weave for us a garment of brightness;
May the warp be the white light of morning,
May the weft be the red light of evening,
May the fringes be the falling rain,
May the border be the standing rainbow.
Thus weave for us a garment of brightness,
That we may walk fittingly where birds sing,
That we way walk fittingly where grass is green,
O our Mother the Earth, O our Father the sky.

ANONYMOUS
NATIVE AMERICAN, TEWA

124

PUTTING THE WORLD TO BED

The little snow people are hurrying down
  From their home in the clouds overhead;
They are working as hard as ever they can,
  Putting the world to bed.

Every tree in a soft fleecy nightgown they clothe;
  Each part has its night-cap of white.
And o'er the cold ground a thick cover they spread
  Before they say good-night.

And so they come eagerly sliding down,
  With a swift and silent tread,
Always as busy as busy can be,
  Putting the world to bed.

Esther W. Buxton

125

UNCLE JOHN IS VERY SICK

Uncle John is very sick, what shall we send him?

A piece of pie, a piece of cake, a piece of apple dumpling.

What shall we send it in? In a piece of paper.

Paper is not fine enough; in a golden saucer.

Who shall we send it by? By the governor's daughter.

Take her by the lily-white hand, and lead her over the water.

At the siege of Belle-isle

I was there all the while,

AT THE SIEGE OF BELLE-ISLE

At the siege of Belle-isle
I was there all the while,
All the while, all the while,
At the siege of Belle-isle.

THE GRAND OLD DUKE OF YORK

The grand old Duke of York,
　He had ten thousand men;
He marched them up to the top of the hill,
　And he marched them down again!
And when they were up they were up,
　And when they were down they were down;
And when they were only halfway up,
　They were neither up nor down.

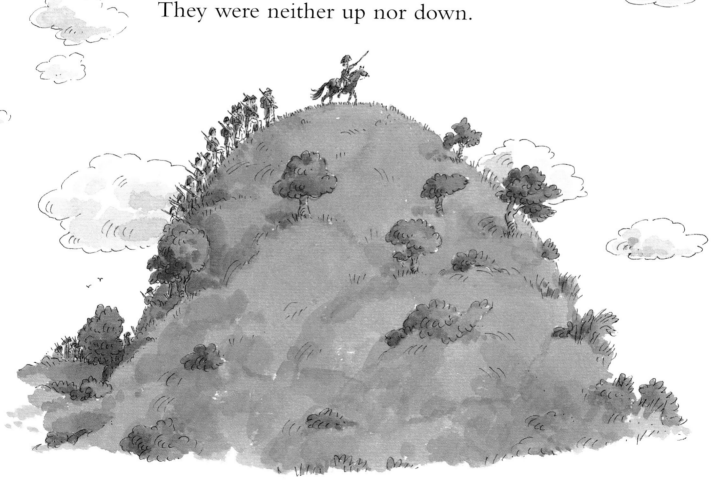

THE KANGAROO

Old Jumpety-Bumpety-Hop-and-Go-One
Was lying asleep on his side in the sun.
This old kangaroo, he was whisking the flies
(With his long glossy tail) from his ears and his eyes.
Jumpety-Bumpety-Hop-and-Go-One
Was lying asleep on his side in the sun,
Jumpety-Bumpety-Hop!

ANONYMOUS
AUSTRALIAN

THE EAGLE

He clasps the crag with crooked hands;
Close to the sun in lonely lands,
Ring'd with the azure world, he stands.

The wrinkled sea beneath him crawls;
He watches from his mountain walls,
And like a thunderbolt he falls.

ALFRED, LORD TENNYSON

129

There was an old person of Harrow,
Who bought a mahogany barrow,
For he said to his wife, 'You're the joy of my life!
And I'll wheel you all day in this barrow!'

There was an old man in a boat,
Who said, 'I'm afloat! I'm afloat!'
When they said, 'No! you ain't!' he was ready to faint,
That unhappy old man in a boat.

There was an old man, who when little
Fell casually into a kettle;
But, growing too stout, he could never get out,
So he passed all his life in that kettle.

There was an old man of Kildare,
Who climbed into a very high chair;
When he said, — 'Here I stays, till the end of my days',
That immovable man of Kildare.

There was a young lady whose chin,
Resembled the point of a pin;
So she had it made sharp, and purchased a harp,
And played several tunes with her chin.

There was an old person of Bradley,
Who sang all so loudly and sadly;
With a poker and tongs he beat time to his songs,
That melodious old person of Bradley.

There was an old person of Jodd,
Whose ways were perplexing and odd;
She purchased a whistle, and sat on a thistle,
And squeaked to the people of Jodd.

There was an old man who said, 'Well!
Will *nobody* answer this bell?
I have pulled day and night, till my hair has grown white,
But nobody answers this bell!'

EDWARD LEAR

SKILLYWIDDEN

A man was cutting furze on Trendreen Hill one fine day, and he saw one of the little people stretched out, fast asleep, on the heath. The man took off the thick cuff that he wore at his work, crept up quietly, and popped the little man into the cuff before he could wake up. Then he carried his find home with care, and let the creature out on to the hearth stone.

When he awoke, the fairy looked quite at home and soon began to enjoy himself playing with the children. They called him Bob of the Heath, and Bob told the man that he would show him where to find crocks of gold hidden on the hillside.

Several days later, the neighbours joined together to bring away the harvest of furze, and all came to the man's house to celebrate the end of their task with a hearty meal. To hide Bob away from prying eyes, the man locked him in the barn with the children.

But the fairy and his playmates were cunning, and soon found a way out of the barn. Before long they were playing a game of dancing and hide-and-seek all around the great heap of furze in the yard.

As they played, they saw a tiny man and woman searching round the furze. "Oh my poor Skillywidden," said the tiny woman. "Where can you be? Will I ever set eyes on you again?"

"Go back indoors," said Bob to the children. "My mother and father have come looking for me. I must go back with them now." Then he cried, "Here I am mummy!" And before the children knew what had happened, their playmate Bob had vanished with his parents, and they were left in the yard.

When they told their father what had happened, the man was angry, and gave them a beating for escaping from the locked barn.

After this the furze-cutter sometimes went to Trendreen Hill to look for fairies and crocks of gold. But he was never able to find either.

ALONE

From childhood's hour I have not been
As others were,—I have not seen
As others saw,—I could not bring
My passions from a common spring.
From the same source I have not taken
My sorrow; I could not awaken
My heart to joy at the same tone;
And all I loved, I loved alone.
Then—in my childhood—in the dawn
Of a most stormy life was drawn
From every depth of good and ill
The mystery which binds me still:
From the torrent, or the fountain,
From the red cliff of the mountain,
From the sun that round me rolled
In its autumn tint of gold,—
From the lightning in the sky
As it passed me flying by,—
From the thunder and the storm,
And the cloud that took the form
(When the rest of Heaven was blue)
Of a demon in my view.

EDGAR ALLAN POE

134

ABOU BEN ADHEM

Abou Ben Adhem (may his tribe increase!)
Awoke one night from a deep dream of peace,
And saw, within the moonlight in his room,
Making it rich, and like a lily in bloom,
An angel writing in a book of gold:—
Exceeding peace had made Ben Adhem bold,
And to the presence in the room he said,
"What writest thou?"—The vision raided its head,
And with a look made of all sweet accord,
Answered, "The names of those who love the Lord."
"And is mine one?" said Abou. "Nay, not so,"
Replied the angel. Abou spoke more low,
But cheerily still; and said, "I pray thee then,
Write me as one that loves his fellow-men."

The angel wrote, and vanished. The next night
It came again with a great wakening light,
And showed the names whom love of God had blessed,
And lo! Ben Adhem's name led all the rest.

LEIGH HUNT

135

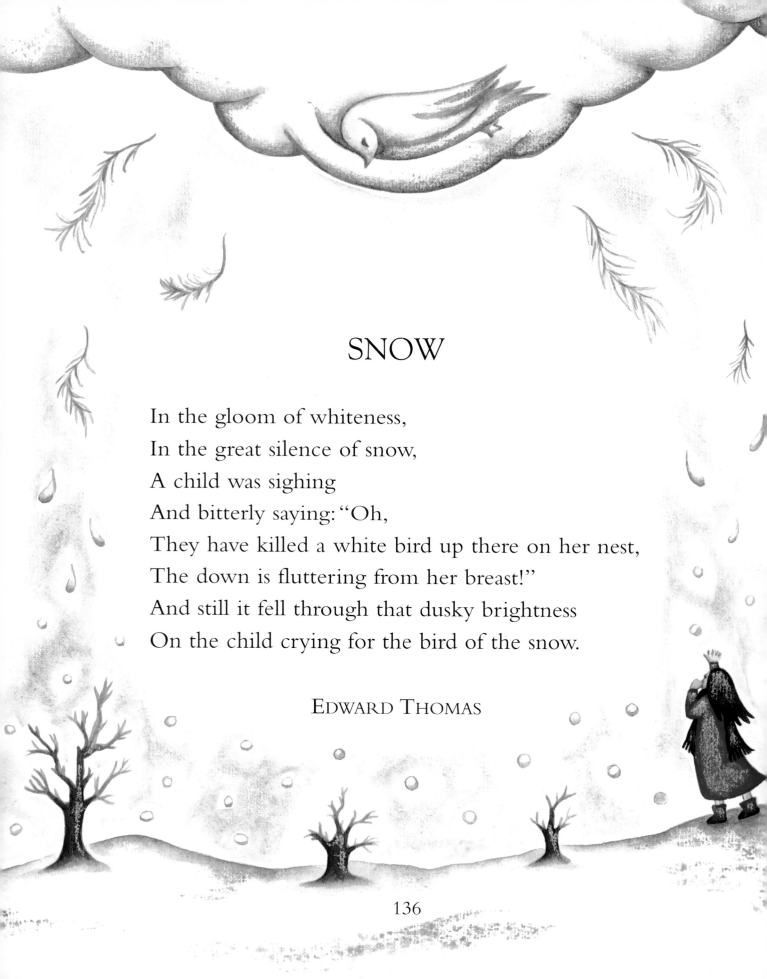

SNOW

In the gloom of whiteness,
In the great silence of snow,
A child was sighing
And bitterly saying: "Oh,
They have killed a white bird up there on her nest,
The down is fluttering from her breast!"
And still it fell through that dusky brightness
On the child crying for the bird of the snow.

EDWARD THOMAS

WINTER

When icicles hang by the wall,
  And Dick the shepherd blows his nail,
And Tom bears logs into the hall,
  And milk comes frozen home in pail;
When blood is nipp'd and ways be foul,
Then nightly sings the staring owl,
    To-whit! to-who!
    A merry note,
While greasy Joan doth keel the pot.

When all aloud the wind doth blow,
  And coughing drowns the parson's saw;
And birds sit brooding in the snow,
  And Marian's nose looks red and raw;
When roasted crabs hiss in the bowl,
Then nightly sings the staring owl,
    To-whit! to-who!
    A merry note,
While greasy Joan doth keel the pot.

WILLIAM SHAKESPEARE

JACK, JACK, THE BREAD'S A-BURNING

Jack, Jack, the bread's a-burning,
All to a cinder;
If you don't come and fetch it out
We'll throw it through the window.

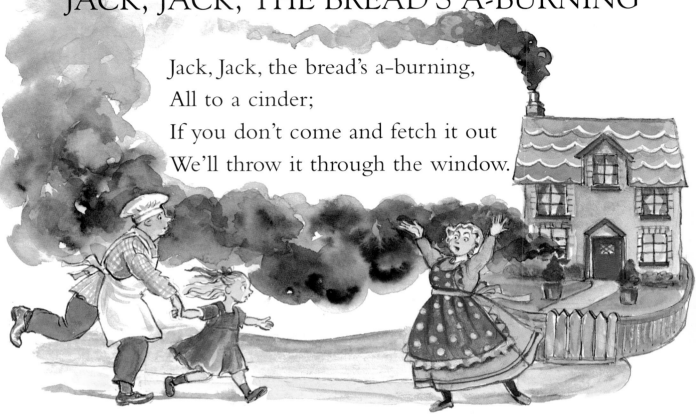

JACK AND GUY

Jack and Guy
 Went out in the rye,
And they found a little boy with one black eye.
Come, says Jack, let's knock him on the head.
No, says Guy, let's buy him some bread;
You buy one loaf and I'll buy two,
And we'll bring him up as other folk do.

138

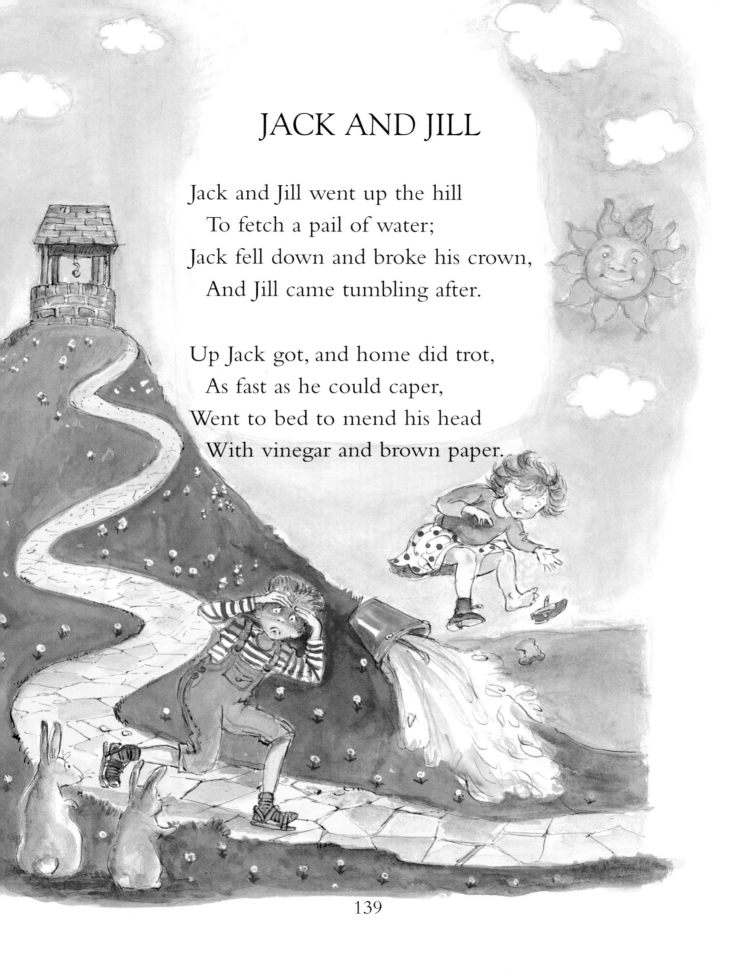

JACK AND JILL

Jack and Jill went up the hill
   To fetch a pail of water;
Jack fell down and broke his crown,
   And Jill came tumbling after.

Up Jack got, and home did trot,
   As fast as he could caper,
Went to bed to mend his head
   With vinegar and brown paper.

TOMMY SNOOKS AND BESSY BROOKS

As Tommy Snooks and Bessy Brooks
Were walking out one Sunday,
Says Tommy Snooks to Bessy Brooks,
"Tomorrow will be Monday."

LITTLE JUMPING JOAN

Here am I, little jumping Joan.
When nobody's with me,
I'm always alone.

THERE WAS A LITTLE GIRL

There was a little girl, and she had a little curl
    Right in the middle of her forehead;
When she was good she was very, very good,
    But when she was bad she was horrid.

THE BLACK LAD MACCRIMMON

There was once a young man called the Black Lad MacCrimmon. He was the youngest of three brothers and he was the most down-trodden of the three. His elder brothers were always favoured by their father, and were always given more food, and allowed more enjoyment, than the Black Lad. The Black Lad, on the other hand, was always given the hardest jobs to do when the four were working together.

The father and the elder brothers were all great pipers, and they had a fine set of pipes that they liked to play. The Black Lad would have liked to have played the pipes too, but he was never allowed. Always the brothers took up too much time with their playing to give the young lad a chance.

In those days, people said that the greatest musicians of all were the fairy folk. The Black Lad hoped that one day he would meet one of the little people and they would teach him to master the pipes.

The day came that the lad's father and his two brothers were getting ready to go to the fair. The Black Lad wanted to go too, but they would not take him. So the lad stayed at home, and when they were gone, he decided to take up the chanter from the set of pipes and see if he could play a tune.

After a while of practising, the lad began to pick out a tune on the chanter. He was starting to enjoy himself, and was so absorbed in what he was doing that he did not notice that someone was watching him and listening.

Suddenly a voice spoke in his ear: "You are doing well with your music, lad." It was none other than the Banshee from the castle.

"Which would you prefer," continued the Banshee. "Skill without success or success without skill?"

143

The lad replied that what he wanted most of all was skill, it did not matter about success. The Banshee smiled, as if she approved of the answer, and pulled a long hair from her head. This she wound around the reed of the chanter. Then she turned to the Black Lad MacCrimmon. "Now put your fingers on the holes of the chanter, and I will place my fingers over yours. I will guide you. When I lift one of my fingers, you lift yours that is beneath it. Think of a tune that you would like to play, and I will help you play. And my skill will rub off on you."

So the lad began to play, guided by the Banshee as she had told him. Soon he was playing with great skill, and he could master any tune that he thought of.

"Indeed you are the King of the Pipers," said the Banshee. "There has been none better before you, and none better shall come after." And with this blessing, the Banshee went on her way back to the castle.

The Black Lad carried on playing when she had left, and he could play all the tunes that he tried. When his father and

brothers returned, they could
hear him playing as they came
along the road, but by the time
they entered the house, the lad
had put away the pipes, and was
acting as if nothing at all had
happened.

None of them mentioned that
they had heard music when they
came in, but the lad's father took
down the pipes, and played as
usual. Then he handed them to
his first son, who played and passed them to the second son.
But instead of putting the pipes away after his second son had
played, old MacCrimmon handed the pipes to his youngest
son. "Now take the pipes, for no longer shall you spend all day
doing the hardest of the work and eating the meanest of the
food."

When the lad played, they heard that he was far better than
any of them. "There is no longer any point in our playing,"
said the father to the two eldest sons. "The lad is truly King of
the Pipers." And the lad's brothers knew that what their father
said was true.

A frisky lamb
And a frisky child
Playing their pranks
  In a cowslip meadow:
The sky all blue
And the air all mild
And the fields all sun
  And the lanes half shadow.

On the grassy banks
Lambkins at their pranks;
Woolly sisters, woolly brothers,
  Jumping off their feet,
While their woolly mothers
  Watch by them and bleat.

O wind, why do you never rest,
  Wandering, whistling to and fro,
Bringing rain out of the west,
  From the dim north bringing snow?

The wind has such a rainy sound
　　Moaning through the town,
The sea has such a windy sound,—
　　Will the ships go down?

The apples in the orchard
　　Tumble from their tree.—
Oh will the ships go down, go down,
　　In the windy sea?

Motherless baby and babyless mother,
Bring them together to love one another.

Swift and sure the swallow,
　　Slow and sure the snail:
Slow and sure may miss his way,
　　Swift and sure may fail.

CHRISTINA ROSSETTI

TIGGY-TOUCHWOOD

Tiggy-tiggy-touchwood, my black hen,
She lays eggs for gentlemen,
Sometimes nine and sometimes ten,
Tiggy-tiggy-touchwood, my black hen.

I HAD A LITTLE HEN

I had a little hen, the prettiest ever seen,
She washed me the dishes, and kept the house clean:
She went to the mill to fetch me some flour,
She brought it home in less than an hour;
She baked me my bread, she brewed me my ale,
She sat by the fire and told many a fine tale.

MRS HEN

Chook, chook, chook, chook, chook,
  Good morning, Mrs Hen.
How many chickens have you got?
  Madam, I've got ten.

Four of them are yellow,
  And four of them are brown,
And two of them are speckled red,
  The nicest in the town.

THE WISE OLD OWL

There was an old owl who lived in an oak;
The more he heard, the less he spoke.
The less he spoke, the more he heard.
Why aren't we like that wise old bird!

THERE WAS AN OLD CROW

There was an old crow
Sat upon a clod:
There's an end of my song,
That's odd!

FIRE ON THE MOUNTAIN

Rats in the garden—catch'em Towser!
Cows in the cornfield—run boys run!
Cat's in the cream pot—stop her now, sir!
Fire on the mountain—run boys run!

BILLY BOOSTER

Billy Billy Booster,
Had a little rooster,
The rooster died
And Billy cried.
Poor Billy Booster.

151

HARK THE ROBBERS

Hark at the robbers going through,
  Through, through, through; through,
    through, through;
Hark at the robbers going through,
  My fair lady.

What have the robbers done to you,
  You, you, you; you, you, you?
What have the robbers done to you,
  My fair lady?

Stole my gold watch and chain,
  Chain, chain, chain; chain, chain, chain;
Stole my gold watch and chain,
  My fair lady.

How many pounds will set us free,
  Free, free, free; free, free, free?
How many pounds will set us free,
  My fair lady?

A hundred pounds will set you free,
  Free, free, free; free, free, free;

A hundred pounds will set you free,
    My fair lady.

We have not a hundred pounds,
    Pounds, pounds, pounds; pounds, pounds, pounds;
We have not a hundred pounds,
    My fair lady.

Then to prison you must go,
    Go, go, go; go, go, go;
Then to prison you must go,
    My fair lady.

To prison we will not go,
    Go, go, go; go, go, go;
To prison we will not go,
    My fair lady.

IN THE TREE-TOP

"Rock-a-by, baby, up in the tree-top!"
    Mother his blanket is spinning;
And a light little rustle that never will stop,
    Breezes and boughs are beginning.
Rock-a-by, baby, swinging so high!
        Rock-a-by!

"When the wind blows, then the cradle will rock."
    Hush! now it stirs in the bushes;
Now with a whisper, a flutter of talk,
    Baby and hammock it pushes.
Rock-a-by, baby! shut, pretty eye!
        Rock-a-by!

"Rock with the boughs, rock-a-by, baby dear!"
    Leaf-tongues are singing and saying;
Mother she listens, and sister is near,
    Under the tree softly playing.
Rock-a-by, baby! mother's close by!
        Rock-a-by!

Weave him a beautiful dream, little breeze!
Little leaves, nestle around him!
He will remember the song of the trees,
When age with silver has crowned him.
Rock-a-by, baby! wake by-and-by!
Rock-a-by!

Lucy Larcom

TWO LITTLE KITTENS

Two little kittens
One stormy night,
Began to quarrel,
And then to fight.

One had a mouse
And the other had none;
And that was the way
The quarrel begun.

"I'll have that mouse,"
Said the bigger cat.
"You'll have that mouse?
We'll see about that!"

"I will have that mouse,"
Said the tortoise-shell;
And, spitting and scratching,
On her sister she fell.

I've told you before
'Twas a stormy night,
When these two kittens
Began to fight.

The old woman took
The sweeping broom,
And swept them both
Right out of the room.

The ground was covered
With frost and snow,
They had lost the mouse,
And had nowhere to go.

So they lay and shivered
Beside the door,
Till the old woman finished
Sweeping the floor.

And then they crept in
As quiet as mice,
All wet with snow
And as cold as ice.

They found it much better
That stormy night,
To lie by the fire,
Than to quarrel and fight.

JANE TAYLOR

157

LITTLE JACK HORNER

Little Jack Horner
Sat in a corner,
Eating his Christmas pie;
He put in his thumb,
And pulled out a plum,
And said: "What a good boy am I!"

WHEN JACKY'S A VERY GOOD BOY

When Jacky's a very good boy,
    He shall have cakes and a custard;
But when he does nothing but cry,
    He shall have nothing but mustard

LITTLE TOMMY TUCKER

Little Tommy Tucker
   Sings for his supper:
What shall we give him?
   Brown bread and butter.
How shall he cut it
   Without a knife?
How can he marry
   Without a wife?

GOING DOWN HILL ON A BICYCLE

With lifted feet, hands still,
I am poised, and down the hill
Dart, with heedful mind;
The air goes by in a wind.

Swifter and yet more swift,
Till the heart with a mighty lift
Makes the lungs laugh, the throat cry:—
"O bird, see; see, bird, I fly.

"Is this, is this your joy?
O bird, then I, though a boy,
For a golden moment share
Your feathery life in air!"

Say, heart, is there aught like this
In a world that is full of bliss?
'Tis more than skating, bound
Steel-shod to the level ground.

Speed slackens now, I float
Awhile in my airy boat;
Till, when the wheels scarce crawl,
My feet to the treadles fall.

Alas, that the longest hill
Must end in a vale; but still,
Who climbs with toil, wheresoe'er,
Shall find wings waiting there.

HENRY CHARLES BEECHING

MEG MERRILEES

Old Meg she was a Gipsy,
   And lived upon the moors:
Her bed it was the brown heath turf,
   And her house was out of doors.

Her apples were swart blackberries,
   Her currants pods o'broom;
Her wind was dew of the wild white rose,
   Her book a churchyard tomb.

Her Brothers were the craggy hills,
   Her Sisters larchen trees;
Alone with her great family
   She lived as she did please.

No breakfast had she many a morn,
   No dinner many a noon,
And 'stead of supper she would stare
   Full hard against the Moon.

But every morn of woodbine fresh
  She made her garlanding,
And every night the dark glen Yew
  She wove, and she would sing.

And with her fingers, old and brown,
  She plaited Mats o' Rushes,
And gave them to the Cottagers
  She met among the Bushes.

Old Meg was brave as Margaret Queen,
  And tall as Amazon;
An old red blanket cloak she wore;
  A chip hat had she on.
God rest her aged bones somewhere—
  She died full long agone!

JOHN KEATS

When fishes set umbrellas up
   If the rain-drops run,
Lizards will want their parasols
   To shade them from the sun.

The peacock has a score of eyes,
   With which he cannot see;
The cod-fish has a silent sound,
   However that may be;

No dandelions tell the time,
   Although they turn to clocks;
Cat's-cradle does not hold the cat,
   Nor foxglove fit the fox.

There is one that has a head without an eye,
And there's one that has an eye without a head:
You may find the answer if you try;
   And when all is said,
Half the answer hangs upon a thread.

O Lady Moon, your horns point toward the east;
Shine, be increased:
O Lady Moon, your horns point toward the west;
Wane, be at rest.

Hope is like a harebell trembling from its birth,
Love is like a rose the joy of all the earth;
Faith is like a lily lifted high and white,
Love is like a lovely rose the world's delight;
Harebells and sweet lilies show a thornless growth,
But the rose with all its thorns excels them both.

What are heavy? sea-sand and sorrow:
What are brief? to-day and to-morrow:
What are frail? Spring blossoms and youth:
What are deep? the ocean and truth.

CHRISTINA ROSSETTI

OLD JOE BROWN

Old Joe Brown, he had a wife,
    She was all of eight feet tall.
She slept with her head in the kitchen,
    And her feet stuck out in the hall.

THE MONTHS

Thirty days hath September,
April, June, and November;
All the rest have thirty-one,
Excepting February alone,
And that has twenty-eight days clear
And twenty-nine in each leap year.

DANDY

I had a dog and his name was Dandy,
His tail was long and his legs were bandy,
His eyes were brown and his coat was sandy,
The best in the world was my dog Dandy!

FUZZY WUZZY

Fuzzy Wuzzy was a bear,
   A bear was Fuzzy Wuzzy.
When Fuzzy Wuzzy lost his hair
   He wasn't fuzzy, was he?

ONE MISTY MOISTY MORNING

One misty moisty morning,
When cloudy was the weather,
There I met an old man
Clothed all in leather;

Clothed all in leather,
With cap under his chin—
How do you do, and how do you do,
And how do you do again!

THERE WAS A CROOKED MAN

There was a crooked man, and he went a
  crooked mile,
He found a crooked sixpence against a
  crooked stile;
He bought a crooked cat, which caught a
  crooked mouse,
And they all lived together in a little crooked house.

ROBIN THE BOBBIN

Robin the Bobbin, the big-bellied Ben,
He ate more meat than fourscore men;
He ate a cow, he ate a calf,
He ate a butcher and a half;
He ate a church, he ate a steeple,
He ate the priest and all the people!
    A cow and a calf,
    An ox and a half,
    A church and a steeple,
    And all the good people,
And yet he complained that his stomach wasn't full.

HECTOR PROTECTOR

Hector Protector was dressed all in green;
Hector Protector was sent to the Queen.
The Queen did not like him,
Nor more did the King;
So Hector Protector was sent back again.

WASH, HANDS, WASH

Wash, hands, wash,
  Daddy's gone to plough;
If you want your hands washed,
  Have them washed now.

CLAP HANDS

Clap hands for Daddy coming
Down the wagon way,
With a pocketful of money
And a cartload of hay.

173

THE FLY

Little Fly,
Thy summer's play
My thoughtless hand
Has brushed away.

Am not I
A fly like thee?
Or art not thou
A man like me?

For I dance,
And drink, and sing,
Till some blind hand
Shall brush my wing.

If thought is life
And strength and breath,
And the want
Of thought is death;

Them am I
A happy fly,
If I live
Or if I die.

WILLIAM BLAKE

LADYBIRD! LADYBIRD!

Ladybird! Ladybird! Fly away home,
Night is approaching, and sunset is come:
The herons are flown to their trees by the Hall;
Felt, but unseen, the damp dewdrops fall.
This is the close of a still summer day;
Ladybird! Ladybird! haste! fly away!

EMILY BRONTË

175

COME TO BED, SAYS SLEEPY-HEAD

Come to bed,
Says Sleepy-head;
  "Tarry a while," says Slow;
"Put on the pot,"
Says Greedy-gut,
  "Let's sup before we go."

176

DIDDLE, DIDDLE, DUMPLING

Diddle, diddle, dumpling, my son John
Went to bed with his trousers on;
One shoe off, the other shoe on,
Diddle, diddle, dumpling, my son John.

177

LITTLE TROTTY WAGTAIL

Little Trotty Wagtail, he went in the rain,
And twittering, tottering sideways, he ne'er got
  straight again;
He stooped to get a worm, and looked up to get a fly,
And then he flew away ere his feathers they were dry.

Little Trotty Wagtail, he waddled in the mud,
And left his little foot-marks, trample where he would,
He waddled in the water-pudge, and waggle went his tail,
And chirrupped up his wings to dry upon the garden rail.

Little Trotty Wagtail, you nimble all about,
And in the dimpling water-pudge you waddle in and out;
Your home is nigh at hand and in the warm pig-stye;
So, little Master Wagtail, I'll bid you a good-bye.

JOHN CLARE

EPIGRAM

Engraved on the Collar of a Dog which I Gave to His Royal Highness

I am his Highness' Dog at Kew:
Pray tell me, sir, whose dog are you?

<small>ALEXANDER POPE</small>

FOR EVERY EVIL UNDER THE SUN

For every evil under the sun,
There is a remedy, or there is none.
If there be one, try and find it;
If there be none, never mind it.

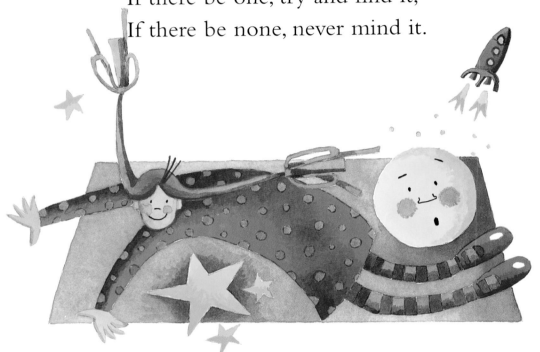

SALLY GO ROUND THE MOON

Sally go round the moon,
Sally go round the stars;
Sally go round the moon
On a Sunday afternoon.

STAR LIGHT, STAR BRIGHT

Star light, star bright,
First star I see tonight,
I wish I may, I wish I might,
Have the wish I wish tonight.

LITTLE JACK JINGLE

Little Jack Jingle,
He used to live single:
But when he got tired of this kind of life,
He left off being single, and lived with his wife.

HARRY PARRY

O rare Harry Parry,
When will you marry?
When apples and pears are ripe.
I'll come to your wedding,
Without any bidding,
And dance and sing all the night.

182

YOUNG ROGER CAME TAPPING

Young Roger came tapping at Dolly's window,
　Thumpaty, thumpaty, thump!
He asked for admittance, she answered him "No!"
　Frumpaty, frumpaty, frump!

"No, no, Roger, no! as you came you may go!"
　Stumpaty, stumpaty, stump!

183

FIVE LITTLE MONKEYS

Five little monkeys walked along the shore;
One went a-sailing,
Then there were four.
Four little monkeys climbed up a tree;
One of them tumbled down,
Then there were three.
Three little monkeys found a pot of glue;
One got stuck in it,
Then there were two.
Two little monkeys found a currant bun;
One ran away with it,
Then there was one.
One little monkey cried all afternoon,
So they put him in an aeroplane
And sent him to the moon.

THREE CHILDREN

Three children sliding on the ice
   Upon a summer's day,
As it fell out, they all fell in,
   The rest they ran away.

Now had these children been at home,
   Or sliding on dry ground,
Ten thousand pounds to one penny
   They had not all been drowned.

You parents all that children have,
   And you that have got none,
If you would have them safe abroad,
   Pray keep them safe at home.

I LOVE LITTLE PUSSY

I love little pussy, her coat is so warm;
And if I don't hurt her she'll do me no harm.
So I'll not pull her tail nor drive her away,
But pussy and I very gently will play.

PUSSY-CAT MOLE

Pussy-cat Mole,
Jumped over a coal,
And in her best petticoat burnt a great hole.
Poor pussy's weeping, she'll have no more milk,
Until her best petticoat's mended with silk.

PUSSY-CAT, PUSSY-CAT

Pussy-cat, pussy-cat, where have you been?
I've been to London to see the Queen.
Pussy-cat, pussy-cat, what did you there?
I frightened a little mouse under her chair.

BOW, WOW, WOW

Bow, wow, wow,
　Whose dog art thou?
"Little Tom Tinker's dog,
　Bow, wow, wow."

TWO LITTLE DOGS

Two little dogs
Sat by the fire
Over a fender of coal-dust;
Said one little dog
To the other little dog,
If you don't talk, why, I must.

PUSSY-CAT SITS BY THE FIRE

Pussy-cat sits by the fire.
   How did she come there?
In walks the little dog,
   Says, "Pussy! are you there?
How do you do, Mistress Pussy?
   Mistress Pussy, how d'ye do?"
"I thank you kindly, little dog,
   I fare as well as you!"

INTERY, MINTERY, CUTERY, CORN

Intery, mintery, cutery, corn,
Apple seed and apple thorn.
Wire, briar, limber, lock,
Three geese in a flock.
One flew east and one flew west;
One flew over the cuckoo's nest.

THE CUCKOO

Cuckoo, Cuckoo,
What do you do?
In April
I open my bill;
In May
I sing night and day;
In June
I change my tune;
In July
Away I fly;
In August
Away I must.

THE LOST KINGDOM

In former times, the best land in Wales lay towards the West. The fertile plains and lush grasslands were fine country for farming, and all who worked these fields grew rich. But there was one problem with the country in the West. The ground lay so low that it was often flooded by the sea. So the kings of the West built a great wall, with strong sluice gates, to hold back the sea. For many years the people of the West enjoyed a life without floods, and they became the envy of all Wales.

One of the greatest of all the western kings was Gwyddno. Sixteen beautiful cities grew up in his kingdom while he reigned, and the lands of the West became more prosperous than before. After the king, the most important person in the kingdom of the West was a man called Seithennin, whom Gwyddno appointed as the keeper of the sluices. Whenever a storm brewed, and the sea threatened to overwhelm the kingdom, Seithennin would close the great sluice gates, and the lands of the West would be safe.

Seithennin was a big, strong man, chosen because he could easily turn the handles to close the heavy oak sluice gates. But there was a problem. Seithennin was a drunkard. Sometimes, when he had had too much to drink, he would be late to close the gates, and there would be some slight flooding. But the kingdom would recover, and no great harm was done.

One day, King Gwyddno ordered a great banquet in his hall. All the lords and ladies of the kingdom were there, as well as other men of importance such as Seithennin. The banquet went on long into the night, and the sluice-keeper got more and more drunk. There was singing and harping, and everyone was enjoying themselves to the full. But because of all the noise of the revelling, no-one could hear that a great storm was brewing up outside. Even when people did start to notice, they assumed that Seithennin had closed the sluice gates and that they would be safe from flooding, as they had been for years now. But no one saw that the sluice-keeper, who had drunk more than anyone else at the banquet, was fast asleep.

Outside, the waters of the sea were pouring through the sluice gates. Soon the fields were flooded and the streets of the towns were awash. But still the banquet went on, until the flood waters poured through the doors of Gwyddno's hall. There had been floods in this part of Wales in earlier years, before the sea wall was built. Then people had lost their lives and good farm land had been spoiled.

But this time it was worse. The water poured in with such speed that it was unstoppable. Men, women, and children, lords and servants alike, were swept under the flood. Even those who knew the sea, including many fishermen who were excellent swimmers, lost their lives. Sheep and cattle went the same way. Soon the whole great kingdom of the West, every field and every town, was deep under the water. And all were drowned apart from one man, the poet Taliesin, who survived to tell the tale. They say that the sigh that Gwyddno let out as he was lost under the waves was the saddest sound ever heard.

The sea now covers Gwyddno's former kingdom, in the place now called Cardigan Bay. Occasionally, at low tide, wooden posts and fragments of stone wall are revealed among the sand, and men say that these are the last remaining parts of one of Gwyddno's cities. Sailors and fishermen who cross the bay say that they can sometimes hear the bells of the sixteen cities, sounding beneath the waves, reminding them of the terrible power of the sea. Some even say that on a quiet, still day they can hear the echoing sound of Gwyddno's final sigh.

HERE COMES A WIDOW

Here comes a widow from Barbary-land,
With all her children in her hand;
One can brew, and one can bake,
And one can make a wedding-cake.
   Pray take one,
   Pray take two,
Pray take one that pleases you.

MISS MARY MACK

Miss Mary Mack, Mack, Mack,
All dressed in black, black, black,
With silver buttons, buttons, buttons,
All down her back, back, back.
She went upstairs to make her bed,
She made a mistake and bumped her head;
She went downstairs to wash the dishes,
She made a mistake and washed her wishes;
She went outside to hang her clothes,
She made a mistake and hung her nose.

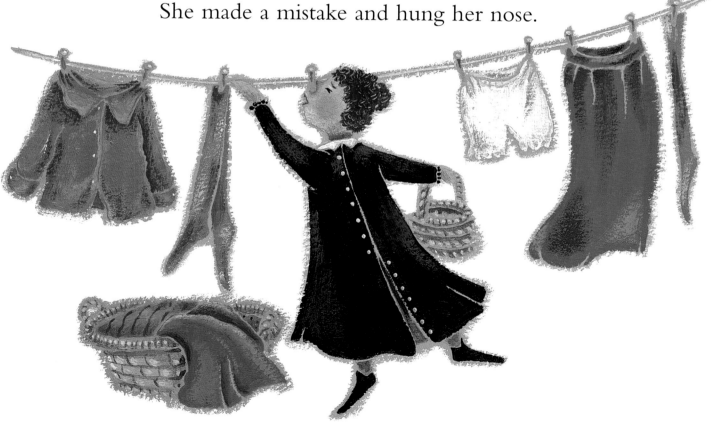

The rose with such a bonny blush,
    What has the rose to blush about?
If it's the sun that makes her flush,
    What's in the sun to flush about?

A white hen sitting
    On white eggs three:
Next, three speckled chickens
    As plump as plump can be.

An owl and a hawk
    And a bat come to see;
But chicks beneath their mother's wing
    Squat safe as safe can be.

Pussy has a whiskered face,
Kitty has such pretty ways;
Doggie scampers when I call,
And has a heart to love us all.

What do the stars do
  Up in the sky,
Higher than the wind can blow,
  Or the clouds can fly?

Each star in its own glory
  Circles, circles still;
As it was lit to shine and set,
  And do its Maker's will.

The lily has an air,
  And the snowdrop a grace,
And the sweetpea a way,
  And the heartsease a face,—
Yet there's nothing like the rose
  When she blows.

CHRSTINA ROSSETTI

THERE WAS AN OLD MAN WITH A BEARD

There was an old Man with a beard,
Who said, "It is just as I feared!—
Two Owls and a Hen, four Larks and a Wren
Have all built their nests in my beard!"

EDWARD LEAR

THERE WAS AN OLD MAN FROM PERU

There was an old man from Peru
Who dreamed he was eating his shoe.
He woke in a fright
In the middle of the night
And found it was perfectly true.

ANONYMOUS
ENGLISH

OZYMANDIAS

I met a traveller from an antique land
Who said: Two vast and trunkless legs of stone
Stand in the desert....Near them, on the sand,
Half sunk, a shattered visage lies, whose frown,
And wrinkled lip, and sneer of cold command,
Tell that its sculptor well those passions read
Which yet survive, stamped on these lifeless things,
The hand that mocked them, and the heart that fed:
And on the pedestal these words appear:
"My name is Ozymandias, king of kings:
Look on my works, ye Mighty, and despair!"
Nothing beside remains. Round the decay
Of that colossal wreck, boundless and bare
The lone and level sands stretch far away.

PERCY BYSSHE SHELLEY

CUSHY COW BONNY

Cushy cow bonny, let down thy milk,
And I will give thee a gown of silk;
A gown of silk and a silver tree,
If thou wilt let down thy milk to me.

I HAD A LITTLE COW

I had a little cow;
  Hey-diddle, ho-diddle!
I had a little cow, and it had a little calf;
Hey-diddle, ho-diddle; and there's my song half.

I had a little cow;
  Hey-diddle, ho-diddle!
I had a little cow, and I drove it to the stall;
Hey-diddle, ho-diddle; and there's my song all!

202

THERE WAS A PIPER, HE'D A COW

There was a piper, he'd a cow,
    And he'd no hay to give her;
He took his pipes and played a tune:
    "Consider, old cow, consider!"

The cow considered very well,
    For she gave the piper a penny,
That he might play the tune again,
    Of "Corn rigs are bonnie".

BLOW, BLOW, THOU WINTER WIND

Blow, blow, thou Winter wind,
Thou art not so unkind
  As man's ingratitude;
Thy tooth is not so keen,
Because thou art not seen,
  Although thy breath be rude.
Heigh ho! sing heigh ho! unto the green holly;
Most friendship is feigning, most loving mere folly:
  Then heigh ho, the holly!
  This life is most jolly.

Freeze, freeze, thou bitter sky,
Thou dost not bite so nigh
  As benefits forgot;
Though thou the waters warp,
Thy sting is not so sharp
  As friend remembered not.
Heigh ho! sing heigh ho! unto the green holly;
Most friendship is feigning, most loving mere folly:
  Then heigh ho, the holly!
  This life is most jolly.

WILLIAM SHAKESPEARE

LITTLE WIND

Little wind blow on the hill-top;
Little wind, blow down the plain;
Little wind, blow up the sunshine,
Little wind, blow off the rain.

KATE GREENAWAY

LITTLE BOY BLUE

Little Boy Blue,
   Come blow your horn,
The sheep's in the meadow,
   The cow's in the corn.

Where is the boy
   Who looks after the sheep?
He's under a haycock
   Fast asleep.
Will you wake him?
   No, not I,
For if I do,
   He's sure to cry.

THERE WAS A LITTLE BOY

There was a little boy went into a barn,
And lay down on some hay;
An owl came out and flew about,
And the little boy ran away.

ELSIE MARLEY

Elsie Marley is grown so fine,
She won't get up to serve the swine,
But lies in bed till eight or nine,
And surely she does take her time.

MARY, MARY

Mary, Mary, quite contrary,
    How does your garden grow?
With silver bells, and cockle shells,
    And pretty maids all in a row.

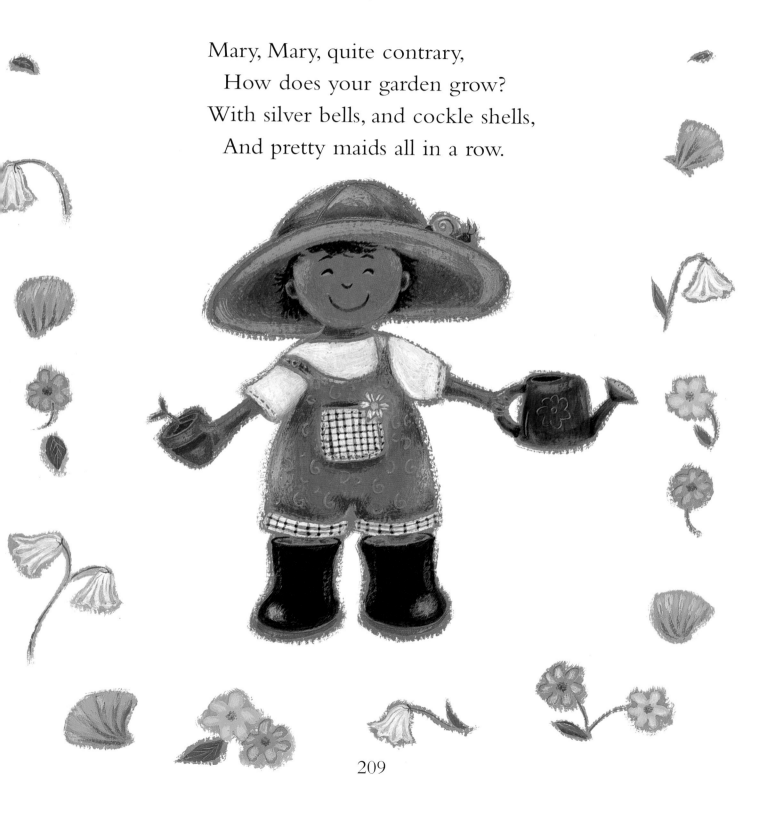

TO A BUTTERFLY

I've watched you now a full half-hour,
Self-poised upon that yellow flower;
And, little Butterfly! indeed
I know not if you sleep or feed.
How motionless!—not frozen seas
More motionless! And then
What joy awaits you, when the breeze
Hath found you out among the trees,
And calls you forth again!

This plot of orchard-ground is ours;
My trees they are, my Sister's flowers.
Here rest your wings when they are weary;
Here lodge as in a sanctuary!
Come often to us, fear no wrong;
Sit near us on the bough!
We'll talk of sunshine and of song,
And summer days, when we were young;
Sweet childish days, that were as long
As twenty days are now.

WILLIAM WORDSWORTH

CATERPILLAR

Brown and furry
Caterpillar in a hurry,
Take your walk
To the shady leaf, or stalk,
Or what not,
Which may be the chosen spot.
No toad spy you,
Hovering bird of prey pass by you;
Spin and die,
To live again a butterfly.

CHRISTINA ROSSETTI

ROCK-A-BYE, BABY

Rock-a-bye, baby, thy cradle is green;
Father's a nobleman, Mother's a queen,
And Betty's a lady, and wears a gold ring,
And Johnny's a drummer, and drums for the King.

BYE, BABY BUNTING

Bye, baby bunting,
Father's gone a-hunting,
To fetch a little rabbit-skin
To wrap his baby bunting in.

213

PEASE-PUDDING HOT

Pease-pudding hot,
  Pease-pudding cold,
Pease-pudding in the pot,
  Nine days old.
Some like it hot,
  Some like it cold,
Some like it in the pot,
  Nine days old.

THE MAN IN THE MOON

The man in the moon,
  Came tumbling down,
And asked his way to Norwich.
  He went by the south,
  And burnt his mouth
With supping cold pease-porridge.

HANDY SPANDY, JACK-A-DANDY

Handy Spandy, Jack-a-dandy
Loved plum-cake and sugar-candy;
He bought some at a grocer's shop,
And out he came, hop, hop, hop.

YANKEE DOODLE

Yankee Doodle went to town,
Riding on a pony;
He stuck a feather in his hat,
And called it macaroni.
  Yankee Doodle fa, so, la,
  Yankee Doodle dandy,
  Yankee Doodle fa, so, la,
  Buttermilk and brandy.

Yankee Doodle went to town
To buy a pair of trousers,
He swore he could not see the town
For so many houses.
  Yankee Doodle fa, so, la,
  Yankee Doodle dandy,
  Yankee Doodle fa, so, la,
  Buttermilk and brandy.

I SAW THREE SHIPS

I saw three ships come sailing by,
  Come sailing by, come sailing by;
I saw three ships come sailing by,
  On New Year's Day in the morning.

And what do you think was in them then,
  Was in them then, was in them then?
And what do you think was in them then,
  On New Year's Day in the morning?

Three pretty girls were in them then,
  Were in them then, were in them then;
Three pretty girls were in them then,
  On New Year's Day in the morning.

And one could whistle, and one could sing,
  And one could play on the violin—
Such joy there was at my wedding,
  On New Year's Day in the morning.

I SAW A SHIP A-SAILING

I saw a ship a-sailing,
　　A-sailing on the sea;
And, oh! it was all laden
　　With pretty things for thee!

There were comfits in the cabin,
　　And apples in the hold
The sails were made of silk,
　　And the masts were made of gold.

The four-and-twenty sailors
　　That stood between the decks,
Were four-and-twenty white mice
　　With chains about their necks.

The captain was a duck,
　　With a packet on his back;
And when the ship began to move,
　　The captain said, "Quack! quack!"

THAW

Over the land freckled with show half-thawed
The speculating rooks at their nests cawed
And saw from elm-tops, delicate as flower of grass,
What we below could not see, winter pass.

EDWARD THOMAS

WEATHERS

This is the weather the cuckoo likes,
  And so do I;
When showers betumble the chestnut spikes,
  And nestlings fly;
And the little brown nightingale bills his best,
And they sit outside at "The Travellers' Rest",
And maids come forth sprig-muslin drest,
And citizens dream of the south and west,
  And so do I.

This is the weather the shepherd shuns.
  And so do I;
When beeches drip in browns and duns,
  And thresh, and ply;
And hill-hid tides throb, throe on throe,
And meadow rivulets overflow,
And drops on gate-bars hang in a row,
And rooks in families homeward go,
  And so do I.

THOMAS HARDY

HAVE YOU SEEN THE MUFFIN MAN

Have you seen the muffin man, the muffin man, the
muffin man,
Have you seen the muffin man that lives in Drury
Lane O?
Yes, I've seen the muffin man, the muffin man, the
muffin man;
Yes, I've seen the muffin man who lives in Drury
Lane O.

OLD ROGER IS DEAD

Old Roger is dead and
  gone to his grave,
H'm ha! gone to his grave.

They planted an apple tree
  over his head,
H'm ha! over his head.

The apples were ripe
  and ready to fall,
H'm ha! ready to fall.

There came an old woman
  and picked them all up,
H'm ha! picked them all up.

Old Roger jumped up and
  gave her a knock,
H'm ha! gave her a knock.

Which made the old woman
  go hippity hop,
H'm ha! hippity hop!

223

THE GREAT BROWN OWL

The brown owl sits in the ivy bush,
　And she looketh wondrous wise,
With a horny beak beneath her cowl,
　And a pair of large round eyes.

She sat all day on the selfsame spray,
　From sunrise till sunset;
And the dim, grey light it was all too bright
　For the owl to see in yet.

"Jenny Owlet, Jenny Owlet," said a merry little bird,
　"They say you're wondrous wise;
But I don't think you see, though you're looking at *me*
　With your large, round, shining eyes."

But night came soon, and the pale white moon
　Rolled high up in the skies;
And the great brown owl flew away in her cowl,
　With her large, round, shining eyes.

AUNT EFFIE (JANE EUPHEMIA BROWNE)

THE OWL

When cats run home and light is come,
  And dew is cold upon the ground,
And the far-off stream is dumb,
  And the whirring sail goes round,
  And the whirring sail goes round;
  Alone and warming his five wits,
  The white owl in the belfry sits.

When merry milkmaids click the latch,
  And rarely smells the new-mown hay,
And the cock hath sung beneath the thatch
  Twice or thrice his roundelay,
  Twice or thrice his roundelay;
  Alone and warming his five wits,
  The white owl in the belfry sits.

ALFRED, LORD TENNYSON

MAGPIES

One for sorrow, two for joy,
Three for a girl, four for a boy,
Five for silver, six for gold,
Seven for a secret never to be told.

LITTLE ROBIN REDBREAST

Little Robin Redbreast
    Sat upon a rail:
Niddle-noddle went his head!
    Wiggle-waggle went his tail.

THE NORTH WIND DOTH BLOW

The north wind doth blow,
And we shall have snow,
And what will poor Robin do then?
                    Poor thing!

He'll sit in a barn,
And to keep himself warm,
Will hide his head under his wing.
                    Poor thing!

THERE WERE TWO BIRDS SAT ON A STONE

There were two birds sat on a stone,
   Fa, la, la, la, lal, de;
One flew away, then there was one,
   Fa, la, la, la, lal, de;
The other flew after, and then there
     was none,
   Fa, la, la, la, lal, de;
And so the poor stone was left all alone,
   Fa, la, la, la, lal, de!

TWO LITTLE DICKY BIRDS

Two little dicky birds sitting on a wall,
One named Peter, one named Paul.
  Fly away, Peter!
  Fly away, Paul!
    Come back, Peter!
    Come back, Paul!

WHOLE DUTY OF CHILDREN

A child should always say what's true,
And speak when he is spoken to,
And behave mannerly at table:
At least as far as he is able.

ROBERT LOUIS STEVENSON

DONT-CARE

Dont-care didn't care;
  Dont-care was wild.
Dont-care stole plum and pear
  Like any beggar's child.

Dont-care was made to care,
  Dont-care was hung:
Dont-care was put in the pot
  And boiled till he was done.

ANONYMOUS
ENGLISH

231

A RARE QUARRY

Two friends were out hunting otters and they walked beside a stream, looking at the banks for holes where the creatures might be hiding. Suddenly, one of them saw a flash of red. The creature moved quickly, darting along the bank and vanishing into a hole near a tree.

One friend turned to the other: "What was that? It was too large for a squirrel, too small for a fox. Could it be a rare, red-furred otter?"

The two men had never seen such an otter before, but could not think what other sort of creature it might be, so decided to try to catch it. They looked carefully at the burrow and saw that it had two entrances, one on either side of the tree. "We'll need a sack," said the first man, and he ran off to a nearby farm to borrow one.

When he returned, he held the sack over one end of the burrow, while his friend stood at the other end and made a noise to frighten the creature out. Sure enough, there was a mighty plop as the creature jumped into the sack. Holding the end closed, the two men made off for home, very pleased with their rare quarry.

The pair walked home across the fields, and had not gone very far when they were amazed to hear a tiny voice inside the sack calling "I hear my mother calling me. I hear my mother calling me." The men dropped the sack in astonishment and watched as a tiny figure climbed out. On his head was a red hat, and he wore trousers and jacket and shoes that were also bright red. As he ran off towards the cover of some low bushes, again he looked like a streak of red, and the men saw how easy it had been to mistake him for an animal.

Looking at each other in alarm, the two hunters ran off towards home. They never hunted for otters again on that stretch of the river.

THE SPRIGHTLY TAILOR

Long ago, in a castle called Sandell, lived a laird called the great MacDonald. MacDonald liked his comfort, and favoured garments called trews, which were a combination of vest and trousers in one piece. One day the laird needed some new trews, and called for the local tailor.

When the tailor arrived the great MacDonald told him what he wanted. "I'll pay you extra," promised the laird, "if you will make the trews in the church by night." For MacDonald had heard that the church was haunted by a fearful monster, and he

wanted to see how the tailor fared when faced with this beast.

The tailor had also heard stories about the monster. But he was a sprightly fellow who liked a challenge — especially if it was going to lead to some extra money. So that very night he walked up the glen, through the churchyard gate, and into the dark church. Finding a tombstone where he could sit, he got to work on the trews, and very soon the garment was taking shape.

After a while, the tailor felt the floor of the church begin to shake beneath him. A hole seemed to open up in the stone floor and a large and gruesome head appeared. "Do you see this great head of mine?" a voice boomed.

"I see that, but I'll sew these," replied the tailor, holding up the trews.

The head paused as the tailor was speaking, then began to rise again, revealing a thick, muscular neck. "Do you see this great neck of mine?" the monster asked.

"I see that, but I'll sew these," replied the tailor.

Next the creature's shoulders and trunk came into view. "Do you see this great chest of mine?"

"I see that, but I'll sew these," said the tailor. And he carried on sewing, although, to tell the truth, some of the stitches were a little less neat than normal.

Now the beast was rising quickly, and the tailor could make

out its arms. Its voice echoed in the stone building: "Do you see these great arms of mine?"

"I see those, but I'll sew these," replied the tailor. He gritted his teeth and carried on with his work as before, for he wanted to finish by daybreak and claim his payment from the great MacDonald.

The tailor's needle was flying now, as the monster gave a great grunt and lifted his first leg out of the ground. "Do you see this great leg of mine?" he said, his voice getting even louder.

"I see that, but I'll sew these," replied the tailor, making his final stitches a little longer, so that he could finish his work before the monster could climb out of his hole.

As the creature began to raise its other leg, the tailor blew out his candle, gathered up his things, and bundled the completed trews under one arm. He made for the door as the monster was emerging, and the tailor could hear the creature's footsteps echoing on the stone floor as he ran out into the open air.

Now the tailor could see the glen stretching in front of him, and he ran for his life, faster than he had ever ran before, for all that he was a nimble man. The monster roared at him to stop, but the tailor hurried on, his feet hardly touching the ground, and finally the great MacDonald's castle loomed up ahead of him and the tailor knew he had a chance to reach its gates.

Quickly the gates opened, and quickly they closed behind the tailor – and not a moment too soon, for as the great wooden gates slammed shut, the monster crashed to a halt and struck a resounding blow on the wall to show how frustrated he was at missing his goal when he had got so near.

To this day, the monster's handprint can be seen on the wall of the castle at Sandell. MacDonald paid the sprightly tailor for his work, and gave him a handsome bonus for braving the haunted church. The laird liked his smart new trews, and never realised that some of the stitches were longer and less neat than the others.

TOMMY TROT

Tommy Trot, a man of law,
Sold his bed and lay upon straw:
Sold the straw and slept on grass,
To buy his wife a looking-glass.

TUMBLING

In jumping and tumbling
    We spend the whole day,
Till night by arriving
    Has finished our play.

What then? One and all,
    There's no more to be said,
As we tumbled all day,
    So we tumble to bed.

BOBBIE SHAFTOE'S GONE TO SEA

Bobbie Shaftoe's gone to sea,
Silver buckles at his knee;
When he comes back he'll marry me,
Bonny Bobbie Shaftoe!

JOHNNY SHALL HAVE A NEW BONNET

Johnny shall have a new bonnet,
And Johnny shall go to the fair,
And Johnny shall have a blue ribbon
To tie up his bonny brown hair.

241

AGAINST QUARRELLING AND FIGHTING

Let dogs delight to bark and bite,
   For God hath made them so:
Let bears and lions growl and fight,
   For 'tis their nature, too.

But, children, you should never let
   Such angry passions rise:
Your little hands were never made
   To tear each other's eyes.

Let love through all your actions run,
   And all your words be mild:
Live like the blessed Virgin's Son,
   That sweet and lovely child.

His soul was gentle as a lamb;
   And as his nature grew,
He grew in favour both with man,
   And God his Father, too.

Now, Lord of all, he reigns above,
   And from his heavenly throne
He sees what children dwell in love,
   And marks them for his own.

ISAAC WATTS

THE BELLS OF LONDON

Gay go up and gay go down,
To ring the bells of London town.

Halfpence and farthings,
Say the bells of St. Martin's.

Oranges and lemons,
Say the bells of St. Clement's.

Pancakes and fritters,
Say the bells of St. Peter's.

Two sticks and an apple,
Say the bells of Whitechapel.

Kettles and pans,
Say the bells of St. Ann's.

You owe me ten shillings,
Say the bells of St. Helen's.

When will you pay me?
Say the bells of Old Bailey.

When I grow rich,
Say the bells of Shoreditch.

Pray when will that be?
Say the bells of Stepney.

I am sure I don't know,
Says the great bell of Bow.

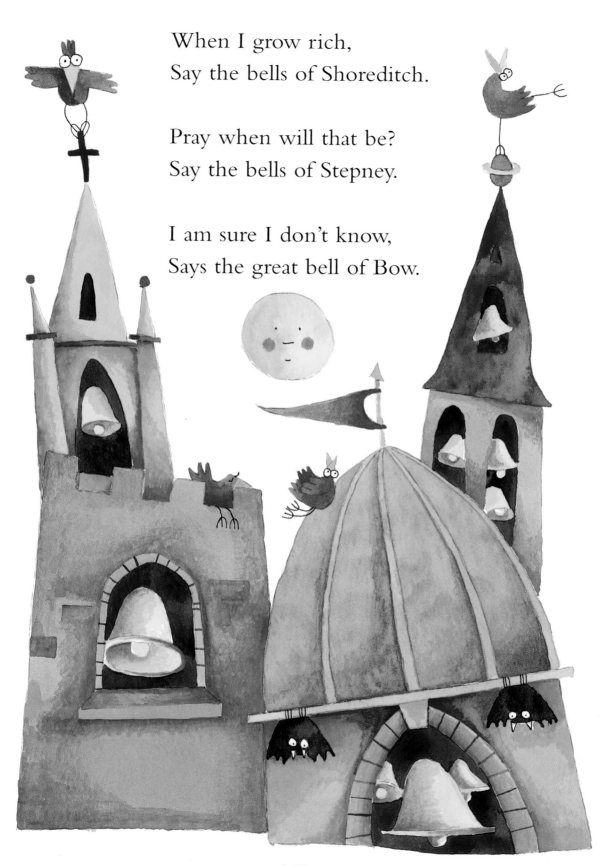

THE TYGER

Tyger! Tyger! burning bright
In the forests of the night,
What immortal hand or eye
Could frame thy fearful symmetry?

In what distant deeps or skies
Burnt the fire of thine eyes?
On what wings dare he aspire?
What the hand dare seize the fire?

And what shoulder, and what art,
Could twist the sinews of thy heart?
And, when thy heart began to beat,
What dread hand? and what dread feet?

What the hammer? what the chain?
In what furnace was thy brain?
What the anvil, what dread grasp
Dare its deadly terrors clasp?

When the stars threw down their spears,
And water'd heaven with their tears,
Did he smile his work to see?
Did he who made the Lamb make thee?

Tyger! Tyger! burning bright
In the forests of the night,
What immortal hand or eye,
Dare frame thy fearful symmetry?

WILLIAM BLAKE

A GOOD PLAY

We built a ship upon the stairs
All made of the back-bedroom chairs,
And filled it full of sofa pillows
To go a-sailing on the billows.

We took a saw and several nails,
And water in the nursery pails;
And Tom said, "Let us also take
An apple and a slice of cake";
Which was enough for Tom and me
To go a-sailing on, till tea.

We sailed along for days and days,
And had the very best of plays;
But Tom fell out and hurt his knee,
So there was no one left but me.

ROBERT LOUIS STEVENSON

THE LITTLE DOLL

I once had a sweet little doll, dears,
  The prettiest doll in the world;
Her cheeks were so red and so white, dears,
  And her hair was so charmingly curled.
But I lost my poor little doll, dears,
  As I played in the heath one day;
And I cried for her more than a week, dears;
  But I never could find where she lay.

I found my poor little doll, dears,
  As I played in the heath one day:
Folks say she is terribly changed, dears,
  For her paint is all washed away,
And her arm trodden off by the cows, dears
  And her hair not the least bit curled:
Yet for old sakes' sake she is still, dears,
  The prettiest doll in the world.

CHARLES KINGSLEY

GOLDY LOCKS, GOLDY LOCKS

Goldy locks, goldy locks,
   Wilt thou be mine?
Thou shalt not wash dishes,
   Nor yet feed the swine;

But sit on a cushion,
   And sew a fine seam,
And feed upon strawberries,
   Sugar and cream.

LAVENDER'S BLUE

Lilies are white,
Rosemary's green;
When you are king,
I will be queen.

Roses are red,
Lavender's blue;
If you will have me,
I will have you.

THE SNAKE

A narrow fellow in the grass
Occasionally rides;
You may have met him, —did you not?
His notice sudden is.

The grass divides as with a comb,
A spotted shaft is seen;
And then it closes at your feet
And opens further on.

He likes a boggy acre,
A floor too cool for corn.
Yet when a child, and barefoot,
I more than once, at morn,

Have passed, I thought, a whip-lash
Unbraiding in the sun,—
When, stooping to secure it,
It wrinkled, and was gone.

Several of nature's people
I know, and they know me;
I feel for them a transport
Of cordiality;

But never met this fellow,
Attended or alone,
Without a tighter breathing,
And zero at the bone.

EMILY DICKINSON

253

A CHRISTMAS CAROL

In the bleak mid-winter
   Frosty wind made moan,
Earth stood hard as iron,
   Water like a stone;
Snow had fallen, snow on snow,
   Snow on snow,
In the bleak mid-winter
   Long ago.

Our God, heaven cannot hold Him,
   Nor earth sustain;
Heaven and earth shall flee away
   When He comes to reign:
In the bleak mid-winter
   A stable-place sufficed
The Lord God Almighty,
   Jesus Christ.

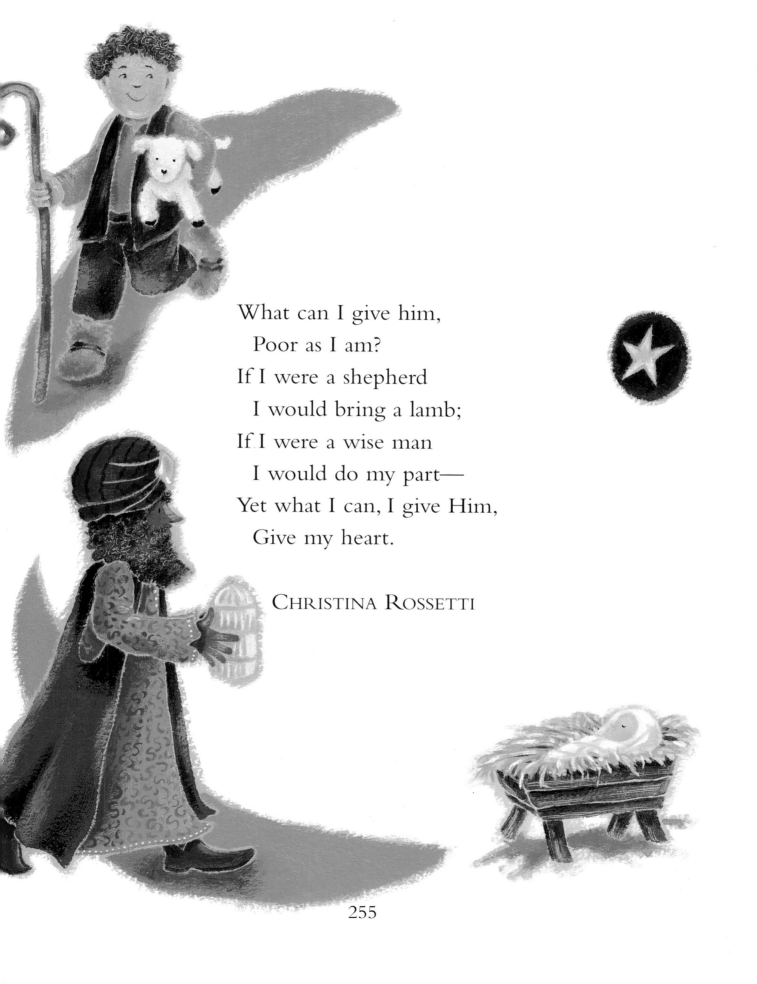

What can I give him,
  Poor as I am?
If I were a shepherd
  I would bring a lamb;
If I were a wise man
  I would do my part—
Yet what I can, I give Him,
  Give my heart.

CHRISTINA ROSSETTI

LITTLE SALLY WATERS

Little Sally Waters,
Sitting in the sun,
Crying and weeping,
For a young man.
Rise, Sally, rise,
Dry your weeping eyes,
Fly to the east,
Fly to the west,
Fly to the one you love the best.